THE
HIGH PRICE

Copyright © 2025 Lora Kay

All rights reserved, including the right to reproduce this book, or portions thereof in any form. No part of this text may be reproduced, transmitted, downloaded, decompiled, reverse engineered, or stored, in any form or introduced into any information storage and retrieval system, in any form or by any means, whether electronic or mechanical without the express written permission of the author.

This is a work of fiction. Names and characters are the product of the author's imagination and any resemblance to actual persons, living or dead, is entirely coincidental.

The views expressed in this work are solely those of the author and do not necessarily reflect the views of the publisher, and the publisher hereby disclaims any responsibility for them.

ISBN: 978-1-917778-97-8

THE
HIGH PRICE

A Novella by

Lora Kay

Also by Lora Kay

Darkness in the Light: short stories
A Woman
A Diary of Unfaithful Stories
London, Love, Life

'Nothing strengthens authority so much as silence.'
Leonardo DaVinci

* * *

'The world will not be destroyed by those who do evil,
but by those who watch them without doing anything.'
Albert Einstein

* * *

'We must always take sides. Neutrality helps the
oppressor, never the victim.'
Elie Wiesel

David had just unlocked the front door to his house, and the aroma of cooked dinner reached out to him. There could be no greater feeling than arriving home at the end of the day. The stress of the last handful of hours would be left there at the threshold, and beyond lay the promise of peace and happy moments with family. David loved his wife and son more than anything in this world. He'd shared over eight years of his life with Mary, and from the very beginning, they'd been blessed with little Chris. What more could a person want from this life? Everything was going smoothly, following the Creator's will.

As a child, David was good, quiet and taught to love their heavenly Father. He grew up as a humble man who had fulfilled his duty – found a wife and carried on expanding the family tree. There were, of course, the everyday obstacles sent by the Divine to test him; for example, a job with a paycheck that left something to be desired, the struggle of handling the bills and so on, but this never truly wore on his spirit. His fate was big, and he knew that whatever plan the Almighty had for him, in the end, there'd be something good awaiting him. This was one of his primary mantras; it was, after all, the very first lesson he'd learned, long ago, when he began his journey, his exploration of faith in the Creator.

Faith, religion, the Creator – the three pillars that sat at the centre of not just David's life but the life of nearly everyone he'd grown up with. In David's town, it was a tall order to find anyone who was an atheist. It wasn't normal. It wasn't acceptable. And most of all, it was shameful.

These pillars were what had saved him through so many moments of weakness and failure, but while he would define himself as a strong believer, he didn't follow blindly as some non-believers would accuse – he simply believed from the bottom of his heart. All in all, David counted his blessings – nothing catastrophic had come to pass through his life yet. He was a humble, honest citizen with a good name and reputation.

Today, Mary was particularly talkative. While setting the plates for the first and second courses, with little Chris's help, she let loose onto her husband a deluge of information.

'I must say that I'm shocked.' She lowered her voice a little as if someone could have overheard them. 'Such a scandal!'

David just nodded in agreement while taking off his jacket and hanging it by the door. Then he went over to Mary, kissed her on the forehead and grabbed the bread to set on the table.

After everyone took their places, Mary had to keep silent for a moment, even though it looked like she was at the point of bursting from whatever more she had to say, but the word now belonged to the head of the family. It was time for prayer. The family would never skip the traditional dinner prayer; it was more than a habit – it was part of them.

'… Amen,' David ended, exactly what his wife was waiting for.

'Can you believe that? She ran away from her husband! Nobody knows where she is. She might even be out of town already. Who would have expected this from Rita? Such a disgraceful act, not to mention the harm this will do to their poor child. Lina is just eleven years old – she needs her mother. Ben is crushed.'

David had already started with the food and wasn't very interested in commenting for fear of missing out on the meal while it was still hot.

'I agree, it's a terrible thing what happened in Ben's family, but the more we talk about it, the more it feels like gossiping. There is nothing to be done for the moment, but I'll talk to Reverend Mark and see how we can all help … It's a delicate situation.'

A sudden sound made the two adults turn their gaze to the youngest member of the family, who'd been sitting silently until that moment. The spoon that was intended for Chris's soup was now on the floor, leaving a smear on the tablecloth and carpet. The child looked scared, and his eyes filled with tears, threatening to run down his cheeks any minute now.

'Chris … what happened?' his mother asked. 'Oh, look at the mess!' she added, getting a closer look at the stain on the tablecloth. She took a napkin and began to dab at it. She would have to wash it, of course, but that would have to wait until after dinner.

'Take a clean spoon, and this time be more careful,' David said to the boy, without making a big deal about it. Children nowadays were so easily distracted, not like those from his generation or even a generation or two later. But one thing was for sure, children were, by nature, naughty and dynamic things, hard to control.

David didn't consider himself a strict parent; for instance, he had never raised a hand to his son. Such a thought was inconceivable to him, even if it could somehow be justified as 'educational'. As far as he was concerned, he and his wife were good people, so how could their child possibly deviate from this same path? There was no need for violent measures to achieve it.

After the short interruption, dinner continued as usual. David talked about his workday, which had gone the same as every other day – a lot of pressure from his boss, who, on top of everything, had told him off again for no reason. 'Some people have no heart or fear of the Almighty, but their turn will come, too.' He loved to say this when he felt indignant about certain injustices. His job was not the best. As an administrator in a small company, his salary only just covered the bills, but expenses seemed only to grow along with their child. Even though children were described as the greatest happiness in the world, it couldn't be denied that they were expensive.

Mary was helping, of course, but her salary was even smaller than David's. After all, working at the counter of a supermarket was neither prestigious nor well-paid. But together they managed somehow. Their hope was that their only son, their pride, would study well and succeed in life. Then he wouldn't have to struggle as they do.

Later that night, after Chris was put down to sleep, David and Mary got comfortable on the living room couch to watch a movie. It was a comedy, and while Mary seemed to enjoy it, David's thoughts were far from the television screen. His arm was wrapped around her in an embrace, and, as usual, he was thinking about how lucky he was to have this woman in his life. At first glance, she maybe wasn't the most beautiful, but when he held his eyes on her and saw every little detail come into focus, oh yes, she was the only one for him. Her long black hair was in strong contrast against her milk-white skin – it all seemed to underpin her seriousness, but once her green eyes smiled at him, David could see heaven's garden.

Mary often braided her hair during the day – she said it was more comfortable, especially for work – but once she got home, she let her hair down, letting it fall in soft waves over her shoulders. It was something David adored; he loved touching her silky hair, which always smelled of flowers from the shampoo she used. She, however, would never know about David's internal playfulness with her hair; he never showed much emotion, the reason for which being something he himself had never been able to answer.

The Creator was his witness for the love he had for his family. David would never want another woman for his wife, and he believed Mary would never wish for another man either, contrary to that woman Rita, whose actions had the whole neighbourhood talking. David would never upset his wife and son like this, but he would also never show his true, complete feelings. Mary had accepted this part of him, or maybe she was hoping for a miraculous change someday. For the time being, however, she would snuggle into him, touch his cheek softly – she would show enough love for the both of them.

Despite being a handsome man, David had close to no self-confidence. Long ago, he had stopped thinking about his looks altogether. So long ago, in fact, that he found himself wondering if he had ever bothered with his appearance. He had faded memories from when he was a child, receiving compliments about how cute he was and how handsome he would be one day. Maybe those comments were flattering to him on some level, but then something had changed. David wasn't sure as to what had changed exactly, but now he made more of an effort to go unnoticed. Besides, there were more important things in life than opening the old drawers of his consciousness – whenever memories tried to conquer his mind, he fiercely pushed them away. As he saw it, the past should stay in the past, and the issues that bothered him back then should be long forgotten. Now he had a family and responsibilities.

This was exactly why he was so happy with his lot; somehow Mary had noticed him, and this thought had always warmed his heart. The day they first met, she was carrying heavy bags of groceries and he was hurrying nervously down the same street on his way to a job interview. At the exact moment they passed each other, one of her bags' handles broke, sending a single red apple rolling down the street. David, of course, helped her regain control over the bag. Mary thanked him and gave what had to have been one of the most charming smiles, to which, of course, he was too shy to respond.

Once he was continuing on his way, he found himself unable to get his mind back on the interview, nor onto anything else. He just repeated to himself how stupid he was for not even asking her name. The Divine, however, had a plan, and later that same week, walking into the packed church on Sunday, there she was. It was more than a coincidence – for him, it was a sign. And that was how it began, with one apple and a meeting in the holy home.

David resurfaced from his thoughts to see that the movie had finished and Mary had fallen asleep on his shoulder. He brushed his fingers softly over her cheeks and smiled. She was sleeping with the expression of an angel. He didn't want to wake her, so he pulled her closer to himself and lifted her to bring her to the bedroom.

When he finally relaxed, lying beside her, he realised that he couldn't bring himself to close his eyes. He was definitely tired, but somehow the exhaustion wasn't enough to push him to sleep. On the contrary, it was as if something was holding his eyes open. A strange feeling had settled in his chest. He had been lying like this, hands behind his neck, for an uncertain amount of time when he heard a noise coming from Chris's room. David instinctively got up in an instant and went to check on it.

When he opened the door of the child's room, David saw his son sitting on the floor with the drawer of his wardrobe wide open in front of him and his bedsheets lying messily on the floor near him. Sensing that he was no longer alone, the child turned towards the door. As surprised as David was to find his son sitting like this in the middle of the night, doing God knows what, it was what he saw in the child's eyes that truly shocked him: fear, real terror, and shame. His concern grew bigger, and with three big steps, he crossed the room and found himself sitting right next to little Chris.

'What's wrong, Chris?' David ran his fingers through his son's brownish hair.

Chris looked down, whimpering.

'You can tell me – you can tell me anything. What's bothering you?' he insisted.

'I was looking for new bed sheets,' the child eventually responded, almost whispering, still keeping his head down.

'Why's that? Your mother had just changed them, no??' Confused, David took another quick look at the mess on the bed and floor.

'Yes, she did, but …' Chris began, but a silent pause followed. David was surprised further to see that the boy's hands were slightly trembling.

David couldn't remember ever seeing his son in such a state. He had noticed recent changes in Chris's demeanour, but nothing like this. In fact, up until now, David had seen the shifts as a good thing. Chris had been the picture of an 'ordinary' child, if there was such a thing, happy and careless like most others his age, with all the energy typical of a little boy. Recently, however, he seemed to have cooled down a bit. David imagined that the discipline of school was a factor. Not to mention he had just finished his first church camp a few months ago. He imagined that all of this must have had a positive impact. Those men who gave sermons at the church were holy people, after all; they wouldn't leave a child twiddling their thumbs with no purpose. They would help the kids focus their energy on reading the holy book. David knew this from personal experience.

As every child in this little town, he'd also grown up with the love of the heavenly Father. This wasn't taught so much in school as at home and at the church. For most parents, it was a relief that the church, on top of the spiritual support, also provided childcare support by organising a few events, as with the summer camps. The kids could learn, socialise and have fun at the same time. All this was well known to David and, as of this summer, to his son as well.

But now something wasn't adding up. On second consideration, Chris's bizarre behaviour and these events didn't seem to fit – they must be unrelated. Earlier this evening, he had dropped his spoon over dinner, and now he was literally shivering and unable to give an explanation. David considered having Reverend Mark talk to Chris.

As for the then and there, it was clear that David wouldn't be getting an answer about the sheets, so he decided to check for himself. He got up and went to the bed to try and solve the puzzle. And then he saw it, a big wet circle. It all suddenly made sense. Chris had wet the bed and clearly felt bad about it. It must not have helped that they'd recently started saying 'you're not a kid anymore', for educational purposes. Now, however, David felt his heart sinking. His own son shouldn't be afraid or ashamed to tell him anything.

'Son …' he started, going back and kneeling at Chris's side, 'do you want to hear a secret?' David went on, beginning to search for a new bedsheet. 'I myself used to wet the bed, often, up until I was even older than you are now. There's nothing shameful in it. You'll grow out of it, believe me.' He smiled at Chris, who had stopped sobbing and seemed to be trying to listen to his dad's words. David, meanwhile, had finally found what he was looking for. 'Okay, let's clean up in here and get you back in bed – it's late. You can have the lamp on for the night if you want.' This suggestion seemed to lift Chris's mood a bit as he nodded and smiled back.

The morning eventually arrived once again, but the day didn't feel as days typically did for David. Apart from the usual unpleasant feeling of another work day lying ahead, he'd woken up with the odd heavy feeling from yesterday still in his chest. He couldn't quite name the sensation; he couldn't even put his finger on what had started it. It was simply there, nearly imperceptible, silently pulsing as though it had its own heartbeat, constantly reminding him of its presence.

* * *

Reverend Mark was getting ready, smoothing out his robe along his body and looking at his reflection. He was satisfied with what he saw, not just with the physical reflection itself but something deeper – he had achieved what he wanted most in life. Mark had met the expectations and hopes of Reverend Simon, who had raised him as his own child.

Ever since his biological father, a known drunk who wasn't opposed to raising a hand to his wife, had up and disappeared one day, Mark's poor mother desperately needed help, and, of course, she sought it out in the holy home. All the same, the news that Mark would be staying under the protection of Reverend Simon, who would be taking care of little Mark and teaching him religion, came suddenly and shockingly. The day his mother had abandoned him – he still remembered her waiting at the front door of the reverend's home, ready to leave forever and without him – had, for quite some time, remained the saddest day in his memory. However, even though she had abandoned him, cold-heartedly, her face, twisted in agony, made it difficult for him to hate her. Her unwillingness to turn around and go that last day was simultaneously a bright memory that often followed the previous and more hurtful one. It had often made him quite sad in his younger life.

Soon, however, the care of Reverend Simon had taken over that and many other unpleasant memories. Mark finally felt protected and loved again, and began to have hopes once more. He owed so much to that man that he'd long ago taken to calling him 'father' and 'family', the only one he felt he had. Mark's devotion and gratitude had no limit, but, unfortunately, no life was infinite, even for the Almighty's loved ones. Reverend Simon's turn to leave this world and join the Almighty had eventually come. Mark remembered how long and fiercely he'd prayed for that great man back then – every day without exception. Now, here he was, already eleven years alone, continuing the great deed of his father.

Mark took another look in the mirror. The robe he was wearing inspired respect in people. It fit him so well, effectively covering the rounded part of his body, a result of 'spoiling', as some people might call it. Not that anyone would dare to say such a thing out loud – nobody had ever said a bad word against the leaders of the church in this town, the holy people who directly served the Creator. Fear was a great weapon, one that Reverend Simon had taught him how to use well.

The event Mark was getting ready for was a baptism. The only interest he had in this event didn't lay in the ceremony but what would be there for him at the end. An unnatural smile crept across his face as he opened his office door to walk out. Nobody would have guessed that his good mood wasn't emanating from the pureness of his heart; the probability that there was nothing holy in him, nothing innocent at all, felt so low – not even Mark would admit the truth of this to himself. He would define himself as a sacred person, chosen by the great Creator, but not in service.

No, definitely not to serve. The world simply didn't work that way – it never had, and history could prove it. The truth was that people were divided into two groups: the weak ones who would always be victims, and the strong ones, who would always survive. They would survive by sacrificing the weak. This was according to the law of nature, and humans simply had to choose which group they belonged to. This was only a piece of the wisdom that Reverend Simon had passed on to Mark over the years; after all, his wasn't just a religious education but an education about life itself.

The ceremony was over much sooner than had been expected – Mark wasn't in the mood to do a proper job that day. He was distracted, sunken into his own thoughts. Preparations for the annual summer camp were about to begin, and for Mark, this camp was a dream come true, a Heaven on Earth that unfortunately only lasted three days, but that was better than nothing. It would just be him and a few fellow reverends, trusted with children of varying ages, whose parents were glad to take a few days worth of freedom while, of course, thinking of their children's important religious education.

The camp would take place in the little hilly area half an hour's drive from town, where, surrounded by nature, the children learned how to love the Divine and how the Divine loved them back. Combining study and games proved to be an effective technique, used by teachers and now those of the church. With the summer holiday coming up, most parents in town would prefer sending their children to the camp, which gave this event a great deal of importance.

For Mark, this would be just another camp. He had attended so many that he couldn't even count them all, but it always brought him the same positive emotion and joy.

After the ceremony had ended and the mother of the crying baby, who'd just been introduced to the religion, had moved down through the big hall together with the guests, the father of the child came up for a final word with the reverend. Emotional, he caught Mark's hand:

'Reverend Mark, I can't express my gratitude.' The man's eyes were watery. 'It was a beautiful ceremony, and now our little daughter is blessed with the Creator's love. You know my family is one of strong belief, and to show our respect today …' The man stretched out his hand for a handshake, but it was obvious his grip wasn't empty. Mark was finally intrigued – the ceremony had bored him a bit, but he always enjoyed this part. He took the man's hand and felt the familiar thrill of paper, which meant only one thing – money. 'A little something from us, the heavenly Father's children, to help you, you who has dedicated your body and mind to a humble life.'

Mark put on his well-rehearsed mask, the expression of a saint, humble and suffering at the same time. 'I am grateful, in the name of all my brothers, not only at this church but all over the world, that our hard work is appreciated and supported by the love of the congregation' – he quickly glanced at the money already comfortably resting in his hand – 'and the help of people.'

The man shook his head as he didn't seem to totally agree. 'This is nothing, Reverend. We would like to give more, but this little bit was all we could put aside after paying the fees for the ceremony.' The man shrugged, noticeably saddened, his shoulders bent from hard labour. 'Our small salaries aren't enough to give more, but if I could, I'd give you a chest full of gold. This church needs repair, and who knows how long you've been restricting your diet. Now, accept this money in our honour.'

'Your hearts are made of gold, and that is what counts, not the money!' Mark said, rushing to end the conversation with this annoying man – he could also feel the gas coming up from his stomach, threatening to reveal his rich breakfast.

He walked away, heading to his office, already thinking about his upcoming lunchtime even though he was still feeling quite stuffed. Once he crossed the door dividing the main hall from the pastor-only section, he looked at his hand to count the cash rolled into a little ball. 'How could this poor man afford to give such a big amount?' he said with genuine surprise. 'I almost certainly own more money than he's ever seen in his miserable life – this must be three times his salary. The fool must have been saving for today.'

Satisfied, Mark put the money in the inside pocket of his robe without a single thought of sharing it with his brothers. He knew that everybody was doing the same thing. This church was a sea of sharks, so he needed to take care of himself. 'If these fools only knew that neither their charity nor their prayers would assure their place in Heaven. For us to survive, they must know nothing of this, nothing of the truth of the religion and the so-called "Almighty". This lack of knowledge is a powerful weapon!' He smiled to himself and entered his office.

* * *

Chris was walking slowly, almost dragging his feet through the halls. Another school day was over, and it was time for him to get back home. There was, however, one problem – the nightmare chasing him from last night wouldn't go away, and the hours spent in classes and the fact that he was about to go home, where he would be even more bored, weren't helping much either. His loss of concentration hadn't gone unnoticed during math class, and if the teacher decided to call home, his parents would likely start lecturing him, which certainly wouldn't help his bad mood.

While walking down the front stairs of the building, Chris noticed something. There was a crowd of students heading to the pick-up area to wait for their parents and get on the buses, but off in the front garden, next to a big tree that Chris suspected was much older than the building, someone was sitting peacefully alone with their backpack tossed to the side. Chris tried to see who it was, but the distance wasn't in his favour. Something about the site of the kid felt distinctly lonely, there was something isolated about them, and this was what drew Chris to them – he'd known something of that feeling recently. He wanted the same thing, to sit alone somewhere to sort through the many thoughts in his head, thoughts that constantly brought him back to his nightmare.

Chris suddenly found himself breaking off from the crowd of students and heading towards the figure. He wasn't sure if he knew the student nor what he might say to them, but for the moment, he found himself craving the company of another like him and being away from the sound of everyone else.

After a few more steps, he could already recognise the form as that of a girl with long hair, now let down, released from the obligatory ponytail, bun or braid. Soon he could tell who it was – Lina, the girl whose mom had just run away, the one his parents had been discussing the night before at dinner. He suddenly found himself slowing his steps; he wasn't sure the girl would want company at a time like this. Besides, she was older than him – what could they possibly have to talk about?

But soon, whatever concerns he might have had didn't matter. The girl unexpectedly turned around and met his gaze, her eyes noticeably red from crying. He felt his insides tighten. It wasn't the fact that she was looking at him that scared him, but something in that look was terrifyingly familiar. It was the same one he saw in the mirror over the bathroom sink, his own eyes burrowing into himself.

'Are you here to make fun of me too? If so, go away or I swear I'll throw a rock at you!'

Chris shook his head and walked the remaining steps between them. Something was telling him she wouldn't hurt him, and apparently a similar something was telling her the same thing. Chris sat down on the grass and threw his backpack next to hers. Lina regarded him for a moment and then went back to her previous occupation – staring into the nothingness.

'My name's Chris,' he introduced himself. A response didn't follow, but it wasn't necessary – he knew her name. This wasn't because they'd ever spoken or had been in the same friend group, and he knew it long before everyone else in town had started talking about her and her family. The truth was that Chris had noticed her long ago.

He didn't like her in the way his father liked his mother – Chris suspected he still didn't fully understand that feeling, and he wasn't in a rush to experience it yet. No, this was something else, something he only felt comfortable saying out loud in the privacy of his own mind. It was her hair. Her long black hair, braided during classes and then let down the moment after the last bell rang, falling freely in rolling waves.

Chris wasn't in the same class as Lina, so he could only see her in the main corridor as the students all found their way to their next classes, but he did see her there, her and her beautiful hair.

Church was the only place he ever saw her outside of school, and the brightest memory he had of her was from the last day of last summer's church camp. Here he was now, sitting next to her, watching the spring wind rearrange her hair with a soft touch. Her presence had actually managed to calm him down a bit; his muscles started to relax, and a faint pulsing headache he'd had for some days started to fade. He knew the reason he was so drawn to her hair – it reminded him of his mother's. Every evening before going to sleep, she would let her hair down the same way, and when she went to kiss him goodnight, the hair would playfully tickle his face, bringing the pleasant smell of flowers. This would always be enough to make him fall into the world of dreams and fairy tales, but not anymore. It was now a memory he'd carry with him, a sweet reminder of a careless childhood.

The silence they both kept didn't feel awkward at all. On the contrary, it was peaceful, almost as though they both needed exactly this – to be alone with their pain, but not completely alone.

'You'll miss the bus,' she said, breaking the silence.

'How are you getting home?' Chris asked, turning his eyes to look at her. She was still looking forward, not seeming to see much of anything.

'My father's picking me up. I think he's scared I'll run away like my mother.' Lina's voice suddenly sounded bitter.

'I'm sorry …' No other words really felt right. Next to him, the girl just shrugged, leaving the silence to take its place comfortably among them again.

Chris, however, realised she had a good point about the bus; he'd miss it if he didn't leave right away, but as he was grabbing his backpack, something got his attention. Between the two of them, almost perfectly in the middle, like a lonely rock jutting up at the centre of the sea, there was a daisy. Had it been surrounded by other daisies, it probably wouldn't have been noticed, but here, awash in an expanse of green, it felt like something special. Chris stretched out his little hand and picked the flower. Then he got up quickly, took his backpack and left the daisy on Lina's.

'Bye,' he said, not expecting a response, but to his surprise, Lina looked at him, her eyes less red this time, and a little smile stretched on her face.

'See you later, Chris.'

The boy ran towards the bus, where he could already see the last student getting on. A few moments later, out of breath and jumping all three of the bus steps at once, he realised there was peace in his mind; ten minutes had passed in which he didn't think of his nightmare, and that was quite something.

* * *

The working day was starting for David, but his thoughts had been drawn in a completely different direction. He was behind his desk, which was covered with folders and documents, all creating little unstable mountains. That is, until an absent-minded move from David sent a lot of it sliding onto the floor. The sudden need to say some not-so-polite words rose sharply in him, but at the same moment, his boss appeared from behind, shaking his head disappointingly.

'David, David … your week hasn't started well with your delayed report, which I'm still waiting for by the way, and now I see that you only continue to be … a disaster.' His boss let an ironic smile split his face and added, 'And you had the gall to ask me for a pay raise.'

With those last words, his boss walked into his office and slammed the door. David closed his eyes, his hands curling into fists. He wanted to punch his desk with all the force he had, and even worse, he wanted to slam his fists right into his boss, who seemed hell-bent on humiliating him. Instead, he bit the already blue knuckles of his hand – he knew a comment in defence of his dignity, let alone a physical fight, wouldn't resolve the problem.

Meanwhile, aggression had been growing inside him lately, with every passing day, like a poison spreading over his mind. It made him hate his boss even more. It was transforming him into a man who he was not. He was a good and humble man; he had never done anything to harm anyone, yet here he was, imagining blood falling down his boss's face.

But violence aside, he needed this job; his family couldn't afford a few months of job searching. Not that he was earning a lot, but things were rough economically more or less everywhere – everyone who had a job, no matter the job, was trying to grow roots there like an old tree.

Suddenly, a heavy hand tapped his shoulder, and David, almost jumping, turned around to see his colleague, Sean. He was just a year older than David and had a refreshingly light-hearted attitude. He was constantly joking around and smiling wide. Somehow, this office couldn't seem to touch him. He even got along with their boss. 'Life for some people cannot be for others,' David mentally repeated to himself.

'What happened here? Did a tornado pass by?' Sean jabbed, even though David was sure he'd seen the whole thing. 'You look like a disaster, Dave. You know what you need?'

'What?' Dave mumbled.

'A disgusting coffee from the machine. I promise you, your day will get better,' he said, winking and wrapping a hand around David's shoulder.

David decided to go along with him, not because of the coffee – this stuff wouldn't even hold up in prison – but because he thought the small moment away from his desk would help him get a grip on his anger.

They both headed to the corridor where the old vending machine stood. David had been expecting the usual pep-talk from his work friend: *our boss is an asshole, don't let it get to you, you shouldn't be afraid to stand up for yourself a little.* But Sean seemed to have something else on his mind this time.

'Things are happening, Dave. My good friend Ben just had his wife run out on him, leaving him alone to take care of their daughter.'

This wasn't news to David, but he didn't want to sound rude, so he changed his facial expression to what felt like something appropriately compassionate and said, 'Yes, I'd overheard something.'

'See? A person can't simply suffer their pain in peace these days. People spread gossip around at lightning speed. How did you hear?' Sean asked, already holding a little styrofoam cup of coffee – the stuff didn't just taste horrible, it smelled bad too.

'Mary worked with Rita, in the same supermarket. When she didn't show up for her shift, news got around quickly.' David was trying to add milk to his coffee, pressing his finger into the old vending machine's milk button until the colour under his nail went white – not all of the machine's buttons worked well anymore.

Sean shook his head disapprovingly, but seeming reassured by the fact that David was already up to speed on the situation, he started to dive into some analysis.

'We need to be objective – we can't just sit here and judge. Who would that help and who are we to do so? Better to try and understand the situation, if it can be done.'

They both leaned against the wall, cup of questionable coffee in hand, and David found himself being genuinely surprised by what Sean had to say. Last night, Mary had put Rita up on a cross, but Sean was actually trying to justify her actions – he was probably the only person in town to do so.

'Ben is a dear friend,' he said, 'and I feel for him, really; being a single parent is difficult. Plus, little Lina is a girl; she needs her mother more than her father, especially at her age. But, at the same time, everyone does deserve happiness. It's what we all dream of. It was more than clear that Rita had never been happy with Ben. He loves her more than anything, but they're young parents and were even younger when they met, just kids, not even graduated from high school, and she was already expecting a child before their last day of school. Their parents rushed them into marriage to save the dignity of their families, and now we're seeing the result.

'Eleven years later, Rita clearly couldn't handle it anymore – she never even had the chance to try out university, for God's sake, or take a step in the direction of any of her dreams. That's a lot. All I'm saying is that I feel pity for her too.' Sean shrugged and then seemed to disappear into his own thoughts for a moment. A few seconds later, though, he shook himself back to the present and spoke, almost whispering. 'This next bit stays between us, okay? It seems that Rita had someone else, like a lover. Apparently, they're crazy in love. Ben started finding evidence all over the house after she left, including some letters. She'd been having an affair for a year until, in the end, they decided to run away together. I don't know if she'll find what she's looking for, but I feel for both of them, Rita and Ben. Their story is sad.' Sean finally seemed done speaking, letting his gaze sink into the carpeted floor.

David felt even more uncomfortable now than last night after Mary had occupied dinner time with the topic. It was such a personal situation, a family drama, something that didn't need an audience; it only needed a miracle, the Divine's help. Once again the idea of talking to Reverend Mark popped into his head, now for both his son and Ben.

'The most important thing to consider is how this is all going to affect Lina. Children are really sensitive; most of the experiences they have at this age leave marks on their consciousness until the end of their lives – it shapes who they are as adults. There's a high danger of trauma.' The subject of Lina was all David felt to comment on.

Sean looked at him, looking a little bit surprised. 'Sure, it's unfortunate that she'll have to grow up without a mother and all, but come on, Dave, she's just a child – they forget fast. And also, who knows, maybe Ben will find a new wife to take Rita's place and Lina will have a woman's presence in the end.' Sean didn't seem convinced by David's concern – he even gave him a bit of an odd look, as though questioning his character more than his comment. 'Can you honestly tell me that you remember anything else from your childhood other than the scratchy knees you got from playing football?'

They both laughed, but something began to bubble uneasily inside Dave once again. If he was honest with himself, memories were certainly something that was missing from his childhood. It all just felt like a large brushstroke of games, school and church … The unpleasant feeling from the night before suddenly pierced him again, right in the chest. It was the same as he'd felt when he found his son upset for wetting the bed. It was once again as though something was alive inside him, pulsing. Was it pain? His hand felt strangely itchy, and he wanted it make a fist again.

This pulsing feeling wasn't pain, it was anger, rage. He held himself back well, keeping the sudden flare hidden inside him, but he didn't know how long he could keep it down – the feeling felt raw, fresh as though from something that'd just happened. All this was scarring him. He didn't want any trouble; all he wanted was a new job and free time to spend with his family.

Conversation over, both men headed back to their desks after throwing their cups of unfinished coffee in the bin. David landed into the familiar feeling of his chair and started putting his desk back in order. All the while, images of his son from last night were firing through his mind: Chris keeping his head down to hide his red eyes and the messy state of the eight-year-old boy's room. It was a mess not too dissimilar from the one on David's desk right now, a mess that had nothing to do with a lack of organisation. It was a mess that expressed anger.

* * *

Someone knocked on the door, and Reverend Mark set down his cup of premium roast Italian coffee, a special order he had delivered regularly. 'People have no shame at this time of the day,' he muttered to himself. 'A person can't enjoy breakfast time in peace; there will always be someone to interrupt.' He didn't even bother getting up and opening the door. Despite the fact that he had a visitor, his unwillingness to interfere with his own breakfast had him carry on with his biscuits, also a special import.

Mark, in fact, had never actually shopped for himself, but he'd not eat from the local supermarket if he could help it. All the same, though the humble life of a pastor was more or less a myth, at least as far as this town was concerned, it was a myth that had to be tended to. So, Mark would send his young helper Tom, who had just turned twenty-one, to buy some bread from the local shop.

Tom often returned with all the money he was sent with and bags full of groceries. A respectful fear of the Almighty earned the big man's representatives some perks, if one knew how to benefit from them.

Mark was a good student of Reverend Simon; it wasn't long before he'd absorbed everything that was away from the gaze of the civilians. The brothers had regular private deliveries of high-quality groceries, including alcohol, cigars, art – for those who were collectors – and many more from a long list of desires and pleasures that a holy man could have.

'Come in,' Mark said over the rim of his mug, followed quickly by a sip as he kept his eyes on the morning newspaper.

Tom immediately appeared from behind the door. This wasn't a surprising visitor for Mark, but he still made his irritation over the intrusion known.

'I apologise, but someone is waiting to meet you, Father.' The young man's voice cracked as he spoke.

'Well then, perhaps you can do your job and tell them as you've been instructed, that I'm in the middle of morning prayers! If you haven't managed to learn your role yet, I'll have to seriously reconsider what use you might be to me.'

'Father, please ...' The worry on the young face wasn't lost on Reverend Mark. 'I know my duties, but something in this man ... I think he really needs help. Please forgive me for the interruption.'

'He needs help ... Do I not have a need for coffee, or breakfast, or peace?' Mark's face turned a shade of scarlet in his irritation. Meanwhile, his assistant stood in silence, head down. Eventually, once he'd finished his barrage, he exhaled audibly to show what a sacrifice he was making for his assistant. He stood up from his soft leather-upholstered chair, went around the desk, which was currently serving as a table for a breakfast banquet, and faced Tom from a breath's distance away.

'Well, Tom, let's see what's bothering this man so much that it was worth disturbing the Creator, shall we?' Mark was using his soft voice now, realising he'd slightly overreacted and had upset his assistant. He lifted his hand and touched the soft freshly-shaved cheek of the young man. Tom immediately blushed and smiled shyly. 'That's it – that's the smile I like to see,' Mark said playfully.

In his turn, the young man lifted his hand and brushed his fingers over the corner of the reverend's lips. Mark gave him a questioning look.

'Crumbs – from the biscuits,' Tom explained.

Mark laughed. 'Yes, it's important to get rid of the evidence before going out there.' The reverend brushed his hands over his lips as well to make sure there was nothing left of his 'morning prayer'.

David was waiting a bit impatiently, shifting his weight from one leg to the other. The church was empty, not a particular surprise for an early morning in the middle of the week, and yet a strange feeling started to crawl slowly over him. He began to feel uncomfortable being there, which was odd considering he came there every Sunday with his family, not to mention all the time he spent there as a child.

A squeaking door opened, and a familiar figure came out. David took a few steps forward and went in for a handshake.

'Father Mark, thank you so much for taking the time to see me.'

Mark had already donned his professional face, that of a humble and wise man of the cloth. 'Ah, child, I'm sure the all-powerful Creator will forgive me for disturbing my prayers to help someone in need,' he answered quietly.

David smiled nervously and cleared his throat. 'I won't take much of your time, Father. I'm actually on my way to work and can't really afford to be late.'

'The world nowadays is moving with such speed, rushing, rushing, and if you ask where to, "to its death" would be the sad but true answer.' The reverend shook his head disapprovingly. 'Money, and the temptations it offers, the thirst for it all has no end.'

'Well said, Father,' David offered, managing a smile that felt even more awkward than the last, 'but I'm not here about the temptation of money – at the end of the day, I just want to be able to put bread on my family's table.'

Father Mark nodded his head and put a hand on the man's shoulder. The weight of it made David's stomach uneasy – he managed not to jump away through force of will. David suspected Mark had picked up on his agitation as he then moved the subject along. 'You're a good man – I see it. The Almighty sees it, but tell me now what worries you?'

David took a deep breath, preparing to get this done as quickly as he could because, for some reason, the unpleasant feeling inside him was growing faster and stronger.

'I'm assuming you've heard about Ben, whose wife just left him, leaving him alone with their daughter,' he started, the reverend nodding thoughtfully along. 'He's really depressed, you see, and I'm sure it can't be good for the poor child. I think if you talk to him, if you can show him the path to the light … maybe he can get back to his old self, for his sake and that of Lina.'

For a moment, the reverend seemed to be considering something, and then his expression suddenly brightened. 'This is a good suggestion. It deserves admiration even. Caring for your brothers and sisters is clearly not something unfamiliar to you, and for this, believe me, you will be rewarded one day! But is that the only worry you have?' Mark caught David's gaze and managed to hold it with some invisible force.

He found himself not wanting to speak about it, and even began shifting his eyes from side to side in an effort to get free from the reverend's powerful stare, which was piercing him right through to the soul.

'I'm worried about my son. Recently, he's seemed distracted … upset even …' Only now that David was attempting to describe his son's behaviour did he realise that he didn't have the words to do so, a phenomenon that felt deeply disturbing.

'The church has the solution to all problems,' Father Mark said. He sounded proud. David knew this was pride in the church, but still, it felt misplaced somehow. He seemed nonchalant, almost happy. 'I highly recommend you bring him in for a meeting with me, and to get him signed up for the upcoming summer camp. He'll spend time with other kids, make some friends and get closer to our great creator than he otherwise could, for three days.' The smile he wore at the end of his suggestion had the distinct air of a salesman, but David tried not to think too much about it – he understood the church had to push; otherwise, things wouldn't change, and people wouldn't do as many of the things they should.

'My wife and I know all about that, of course, but I—'

'Great, then it's all settled. I'll add you to the list.'

David blinked a few times, confused. He was pretty sure he wasn't about to sign up when he started his answer. The unpleasant feeling inside him had suddenly taken the shape of an angry ocean wave, overtaking him, but for the life of him, he couldn't understand why this emotion was flaring up so much at this time. He could understand it surfacing at work, but the church was normally a place of relaxation, community and family. His delay in response and subsequent facial expression must have given something of his doubt away.

'Am I to understand that you're not willing to give your son a moment closer to the Almighty?' Father Mark finally said, and David suddenly became aware of the fact that he'd been quiet for some time, at least half a minute, and his face must have been doing something weird.

The tone Father Mark had used in his last comment was reproachful, and David understood that he had no choice. He never had one, actually. Here, it wasn't considered 'normal' to wilfully be a stranger to religion – it was something to be followed without question. This was a tradition that went back through the ages, and even though modern principles have tried countless times to break the habit of the great Creator, known as 'God' by some and by many other names by many other people, it seems that the effort has been in vain. As long as the believers and religious followers had some, any, advantage over those who didn't follow, the general public opinion of the latter would always be one of lunacy, and this was true for David's town, and he respected this unspoken law. He believed. This made it sting all the more when Father Mark questioned his devotion.

'No, of course not. How could I …' the man said, shaking his head in denial.

'Fantastic. We'll get him added to the list and I'll expect your son for a private consultation on Friday after school. Now, if you'll excuse me, my job awaits, yours as well, I believe.'

David was sure he could still sense doubt in Father Mark's eyes, doubt about the integrity of his faith. He felt certain that the abrupt end to their meeting meant he'd offended the man – it didn't help in the way of his emotional uneasiness.

He headed to the exit, thinking over Father Mark's reaction. The whole thing made him feel small, insignificant, and ashamed. Who was David to disagree with the word of this holy man? But at the same time … who made this man holy? Did that power belong to a human? This question struck with such speed that David didn't have time to suppress it in his mind. It echoed in his consciousness as something forbidden, something that had just managed to slip out of the box and was trying to spread its wings before they could be cut off. It was thirsty for attention, for freedom … The knuckles of David's hands turned white once again under the squeezing pressure of his fists. His hands simply couldn't relax, so he hid them in the pockets of his coat.

Today was supposed to have started well. The idea of helping poor Ben had occurred to him so suddenly, and this visit was supposed to have left him with a nice feeling, the feeling of doing something good. Instead, his lungs seemed unable to fill with enough air, and his chest felt heavy, as though a bag of stones had been placed on it. Meanwhile, his vision was noticeably blurry, not from tears but from the returning pulse of his headache … The image of his boss appeared in his mind as though summoned, and David suddenly knew exactly what would release the pressure valve of his emotional tank – to see blood on that man's face.

* * *

It was the end of the week, or at least the school week, and Chris was looking forward to the weekend when he could rest at home. At the same time, he could feel impatience for it to be over, so that he could see Lina again. The last time he saw her was, in fact, the first time they had ever talked. Just a few words were exchanged, but the amount wasn't important. What mattered was how being with her had made him feel. He felt so completely at peace, his mind firmly taken away from his nightmares. 'Maybe I'll see her this Sunday at church,' he hoped.

Chris knew that if he were to share these thoughts out loud, he would almost certainly be made fun of, accused of liking her and wanting her to be his girlfriend. That's why he'd never mention it to anybody. Besides, this wasn't even true. He didn't even like girls yet – his mind was still more focused on computer games and LEGO – but since his nightmares had started a year ago, he'd been trying to get rid of them in any way possible, but this had proved unsuccessful. That day in the school garden, however, Lina had made him forget for just a little bit. How nice it was to feel like himself again, just a kid, breathing freely without an invisible weight on his chest, able to relax the muscles of his face, which had more frequently been twisting into a mask of fear.

Chris got off the school bus and headed to his house at the end of the street. It was a sunny day, though not really hot, as the summer was still a little over a month away. The trees were covered in blossoms and the air was filled with the sweet smell of spring. The sun felt gentle, almost soft, but still warm. For a moment, he'd almost felt lighter.

When he opened the front door, he found his mother watering a small plant they had in the corridor.

'Hey, sweetheart.' She smiled at him and set the watering can to the side, coming over to kiss him on the forehead. Her hair was tied in a bun, preventing it from falling in the usual tickling way that Chris liked so much.

He was actually a bit surprised to find her home at this time of day, but before he could ask, she started moving them along – she seemed in a hurry.

'Come have lunch. You'll have to eat quickly, I'm afraid – we have to get going.'

The child did what he was told and followed her to the kitchen, but he was still confused as to what was going on. 'Where are we going, Mom?' Chris said, taking a seat at the table.

His mom had begun ladling soup into a bowl. When she turned around, she seemed surprised. 'Did your father not tell you? You're going to have a visit with Reverend Mark.' She put the bowl on the table and turned back to the kitchen countertop, still talking as she chopped some vegetables. 'I'll be here getting some dinner things going while you eat – I have to go finish my shift at the supermarket right after I drop you at the church. Your father will pick you up afterwards.'

She was talking a lot, as she usually did. She didn't even notice that Chris hadn't said a word after she served him. Usually, this just meant he was digging in, so she didn't think much of it.

After about ten minutes, she'd already finished preparing the vegetables and turned back to check on her son. To her surprise, his hands were on his lap, and everything in front of him was exactly as she'd placed it. She frowned. 'Chris ... honey, are you alright?' she asked, worried at first, but when he nodded, after a brief moment of relief, she was upset. 'Why haven't you eaten then?'

Chris just shrugged.

'Well, you should have at least told me if you weren't hungry. We could have saved some time. Come on, go get your jacket,' she said, taking the bowl of soup and putting it in the fridge.

Chris listened, but he certainly didn't hurry. Rather, he dragged his feet. It felt like all he could do. He didn't want to go to the meeting, but as his mom had told him a thousand times, children didn't have a say in important decisions like this. He told himself that would change once he grew up. Yes, then he would be in charge of his own decisions. Then nobody would force him to do things ...

Eventually, after some more prodding from his mother, they were both out of the house and headed to the bus stop. The church was no more than fifteen minutes away, but the time Mary was allotted to get her son there was running out fast. It wasn't easy for her, always having a lack of time, doing everything quickly, intensely, fighting to save a minute or two while all the housework was always waiting on her. But that was life, and she had accepted it as it was, and now she worried something was going on with her son – she didn't even have time to find out what it could be. On the other hand, who better to get to the bottom of this than Father Mark?

Mary switched her gaze from her watch to her son and then back again. She loved her child so much, flesh and blood, her own creation made in her image, part of her ... Thinking about it made her feel all the closer to the heavenly Father. She gave her head a small shake to help bring her back to the moment and away from such ridiculous thoughts – she nearly just compared herself to the great Creator himself. She imagined that not even direct servants of the Almighty would dare to do such a thing as she, a simple woman, had nearly done.

She had grown up with religion, but if she had to be completely honest – something she could only be in her own mind – she never really had a choice but to be religious. Over time, idolising the belief had become a habit, and then part of her life. Sometimes, very late at night, when she was having trouble falling asleep, strange thoughts would find their way into her mind and scare her, terrify her with such a gripping fear that because of such self-honesty she would burn in Hell for all eternity.

She felt she wouldn't be following her husband to Heaven, where he would certainly go. David was very religious. She knew this, even though they never discussed it much. Even though they went to church as a family every Sunday, they still didn't talk about it much, apart from the occasional discussion about certain church obligations. Maybe there really wasn't that much to discuss. After all, it was something to take on faith, so what was there to debate? If one didn't fully embrace religion, they might soon feel her swift kick in the form of side glances, talks behind one's back, and finally, exclusion – the doubter was something to be removed, not cured. Yes, it was certainly better, and easier, to follow the footsteps of those walking directly in front of oneself.

Chris's mom exhaled and took his hand in hers as they got off the bus. They hadn't a great distance to travel, but still, for Chris, it felt as though they'd flown. His mother was in a hurry, so she didn't have time to notice he was dragging his feet all the more. When they finally arrived, a man with a bent spine welcomed them. He'd always scared Chris, and now was no exception as he moved to hide behind his mother.

'Father Mark is expecting us,' Mary said quickly.

'That's fine. He should be here shortly,' the man said, moving off to continue sweeping the floor.

Mary took a big exhale, not bothering to hold back the sound of it, and looked back at her watch. 'Do you have an idea of how long it will take?' she called after the man.

He turned around to take another look at the visitors. He seemed to pick up on the fact that time was something they didn't have.

'Unfortunately, ma'am, I can't say precisely. Maybe about ten minutes?' He hesitated for a second and then offered, 'Is there anything I can help you with?'

'Actually … I'm running a bit late for work, and my son has a meeting with Father Mark, and maybe if …' She trailed off, leaving the sentence intentionally open to see how much the man was willing to help.

'It's not a problem if you want to leave the child with me. I'll keep an eye on him.'

This was exactly what Mary wanted to hear. 'Oh, thank you so much! That'd be a really big help,' she said, already turning to Chris for final instructions. She found him with eyes wide, looking horror-stricken, shaking his head adamantly in disapproval.

She pulled him over to the side and kneeled in front of him. 'Don't be silly. There's nothing to be afraid of. You're in the Father's house! It's the safest place for a child. Now, I want you to be a very good boy and behave yourself, as we taught you, and I don't want to hear any complaints from the reverend afterwards. This would upset your father and me – you'd embarrass us. Are we clear?' she asked, using her stern voice.

Chris hated her stern voice. He knew better than to disobey it, but this was largely because he loved his mother and didn't want to see her upset or disappointed. Plus, he was well aware that he didn't have much of a choice.

He nodded silently, and that seemed to be enough for his mother. She kissed his forehead and thanked the man with the broom once again as he continued his work along the floor.

'Your father will be here in an hour, when he finishes work.' This was the last thing she said, then she disappeared from the child's sight.

Chris held both his hands in front of him and stared at his shoes. He was confused and scared. He had no idea what reason could warrant a visit to the church, but there he was, at church, with a scary man who looked like he might want to hurt him.

He was certain this had to be a punishment of some kind, and he quickly began thinking over all the different things he'd done that could have gotten him in trouble. Could it be for the other night, when he wet the bed? Or maybe because he hadn't heard the teacher's question in class and made her repeat herself. A little voice inside his head was telling him he'd done nothing wrong, but his conscience said otherwise – if his parents were allowing it, maybe he did deserve to be punished. They had no problem leaving him there, all alone with the scary-looking man, nor to send him off to Father Mark. So, even if he couldn't understand the reasons, he must have deserved this somehow.

'Hey boy,' the man with the broom said, 'don't stand there like that. Go have a seat and get comfortable.' His face stretched into something resembling a smile. Then he pointed to a line of old wooden chairs by the wall.

At that moment, a soft, familiar voice floated between them. 'James, though your intentions were kind, I think you've scared our little guest,' Father Mark said, smiling down at Chris.

'Forgive me, Father ... I was just saying that the weather is so lovely today. Best to do one's duty outside, under the sun, if one can. Better than doing so behind these heavy stone walls ...' James said, confusing Chris as he'd been saying nothing like that.

'Instead of thinking of others' jobs, I suggest you think of yours! You have sweeping to do – less talking.' The reverend's voice was sharp, as it was no doubt intended to be. No regret showed on his face for speaking that way to James.

Chris looked at the old cleaner, who had looked scary up until that point, and tried to figure out why he lied. While he and Father Mark continued to share a silent, intense moment, something in James's face seemed to soften, and Chris felt differently towards him all of a sudden, as though he were now seeing him with different eyes.

'This way, Chris,' the reverend said, offering his hand, which Chris knew to be waiting for his. He begrudgingly did what was expected of him, and the two began making their way out of the main room. Chris took one last look over his shoulder at the old cleaner by the front door, and to Chris's surprise, the man was looking back. There was something sad about the way he watched on.

Exactly one hour later, little Chris was walking back the same way. He held one hand in his pocket, the nail of his pointer finger digging sharply into the skin of its neighbour. It hurt. Chris wanted it to hurt – it kept the tears in and his thoughts where he wanted them, on the pain and not elsewhere. The reverend was there with him, walking him the short distance from his office to the front door, where his father was already waiting.

When they came to a stop, his dad greeted Father Mark with a handshake and then reached out to ask for his own hand. Chris was feeling relieved that the visit was over and that his father was finally there, but he still didn't say a word.

'Wait for me outside,' his dad said. 'I'll be with you in a minute.'

Chris turned and was heading gratefully towards the door when his father stopped him. 'Chris, where are your manners? Don't you have anything to say to Father Mark?' Then he turned back to the reverend. 'I'm sorry about this, he doesn't normally forget to thank.'

The reverend was waiting there with a soft smile, but Chris remained silent. It was like he had something stuck in his throat, blocking the words from coming out. Eventually, after the pressure of his father's look increased, he managed a weak 'goodbye' and ran out.

Outside, the weather was still warm, even though the sun was already hiding its last rays. The chilling air could be felt a bit more, but for Chris, it was refreshing. He stopped in front of a bush on which a little butterfly had landed. Fluttering with its pastel wings, it looked like a drop of beautiful colour on the green bush. Chris had seen kids at school catching butterflies and torturing them by tearing their wings. The children's laughter would shriek through the air as they inflicted pain. For Chris, this was far from entertainment. In fact, he found it unbearable to watch. He knew he wasn't particularly strong, and that the other kids would only hurt him if he tried to stop them. He lacked courage, so he simply turned a blind eye, but inside, the word 'Stop!' always boiled in his chest. It was a feeling he'd been having more and more lately.

Just inside the door of the church, David was thanking Father Mark for his time and talking over the meeting a little while Chris was off on his own. 'So, is he alright? Could you gather anything about what's bothering him?' he asked, hoping that, whatever it was, it wouldn't be so bad that Mary wouldn't be able to deal with it.

The Reverend let out a heavy exhale and furrowed his eyebrows, the empathetic air of a doctor just before they gave bad news. 'To be honest, I'm a little bit surprised; the boy seems to take religion very lightly. He doesn't seem to be as well instructed in the love of our Father as I would have hoped.'

David did what he could to hide his shock from the accusation, but he feared he wasn't doing a very good job of it. 'But—' he started, but his objection was immediately cut off by the look of indignation that came over Father Mark's face.

'For this,' Father Mark said, launching right back in, 'I highly recommend regular visits with me. It's a good thing you've already enlisted him in this year's summer camp. This is, after all, the boy's soul we're talking about – it isn't to be taken lightly. When it comes to the mercy of the Almighty, our hearts and our time are a small cost. Don't you agree?' Mark ended his speech with a smile, which felt oddly inappropriate to David.

David stood there for a moment, looking at Father Mark, and then he simply nodded in agreement.

'Well, I don't want to keep you any longer, Father, so I'll just wish you a pleasant evening and be on my way, and again, thank you for your help.' David was well aware of the effort needed to keep up his good manners, to cover up his own discomfort he had from being around the reverend.

He gave a small half wave and another attempt at a smile and then turned for the door. In just a handful of large steps, he was at his son's side. 'Let's go home,' he said, wrapping his arm around the child's shoulders and leading them towards the gate.

There was no need to rush. They were in no hurry. There was no need for them to leave the church grounds at a near run, but David could feel goosebumps beginning to spread over his entire body.

Both of David's feet nearly left the ground when their path was suddenly cut off by someone. After the initial shock wore off, David saw that it was the old cleaner with a rusty watering can, going about the plants. He stood there a moment, staring at them, not saying anything. David stood there in silence as well, expecting him to say something. Then he smiled and nodded in the manner of someone wishing someone goodbye and made to go around the man.

As they continued away, Chris turned to look once again at the man. His eyes were the same as before, sad, like the neighbourhood's stray kitten – people had told Chris there was no need to pity the little cat as everyone was apparently feeding it, but that didn't keep a stabbing sadness from Chris's chest every time he saw it. He found the same sadness filling his chest as he watched the old man. Then just as Chris was about to turn away, the man moved his lips, silently offering a parting message – 'I'm sorry …'

* * *

That evening's dinner was quiet. Nobody seemed in the mood for conversation. Usually, Mary would be the one to fill the space, but even she seemed to have reached the limits of her energy. David thought about what the other two members of his family could be thinking, and he wondered if they had an idea of what was going through his own mind.

He would have traded just about anything at that moment to quash his current thoughts. His mind kept shooting back to the discomfort he felt while talking to the reverend that afternoon and the pulsing pain he felt – the same pain that had his hands in fists back at the office. He felt like something was happening, but he hadn't the slightest idea of what it could be.

His mind felt chaotic, and it was ruining his appetite. David looked at his son. The kid had broken a slice of bread into small pieces but wasn't eating it. His fork was making noise on the plate, but he wasn't picking up any food; he was only arranging pieces of potato into a line and then destroying it. Apparently, the lack of appetite was shared.

After dinner had finished, David sat comfortably on the couch in the living room and started checking the TV channels for something interesting. Mary was getting Chris ready for bed, which usually included telling a bedtime story from his favourite book after the long drawn-out process of brushing teeth and getting changed.

David eventually found a movie that held his interest. In the first three minutes, it had given the impression of a typical romantic comedy, but a quick scene change shifted the mood as two men were shown sharing a passionate kiss. David grabbed the remote and turned off the television. It wasn't that he minded or had ever frowned upon any of the forms love took, but there was something he couldn't quite explain within himself that triggered him in that moment.

What's more, he could feel the taste of his dinner coming up from his stomach, threatening to erupt. The sudden feeling was so strong that he had no other choice but to run to the toilet with his hand covering his mouth. The moment he slammed the door behind his back and kneeled in front of the toilet, his wife's worried voice came from the other side of the door.

'Darling, is everything alright?'

Given the sudden lack of privacy, he shook off whatever had disturbed him – through some effort – deciding he'd leave no room for weakness. He took a deep breath. 'The potatoes are just sitting a little heavy. My stomach is a bit upset.'

'Hm, I didn't do anything differently; I cooked them as I usually do. Are you sure you haven't picked up some sort of flu? A colleague of mine complained of some stomach pain today … I just don't want Chris to get it.' Mary was nervously biting her lip at the idea of spending the weekend taking care of her ill husband and son when she so desperately needed a break herself.

'I hope not,' answered David, already getting to his feet. The feeling had gone as suddenly as it came. He reached for the door handle, ready to come out and assure his wife, when he was struck by the sudden jolt of a memory, ripping through his mind, up from God knew where. As a child, he used to sit in front of the toilet just like this, vomiting and crying.

* * *

Even though the sun had long since gone down, Father Mark was still in his office, quite focused on his work. He peered through his glasses, forehead bunched in concentration as he scratched something down in his notebook. His state of absorption went on for another few minutes until he was ripped back up to the surface by the sound of someone knocking at his door, followed swiftly by the appearance of Tom's handsome young face.

'May I?' he asked.

'Of course,' Mark replied, setting his glasses on the desk and looking at the young man with a soft smile.

'I wanted to offer some assistance with whatever is keeping you so busy so late,' Tom said, circling around the desk and stopping close to Mark, inappropriately close for a professional relationship. This may have offended someone else, but not Mark – he was used to the closeness of his assistant; in fact, he enjoyed it.

'I'm organising the upcoming camp. The small details are the biggest headache.' He exhaled and let himself close his heavy eyelids for a moment. Time had been fairly kind to him – his body was decently strong and capable – but some small health issues that came with age did, on occasion, exact their toll. He was still fairly young, fifty-four years old, but did find himself requiring the aid of a few pills from time to time to keep some of the more intrusive symptoms off him.

His doctor had warned him many times about the risks that came with the regular consumption of meat, the drinking of wine, and the smoking of cigars, but he didn't listen as much as he maybe should have. He could feel fatigue sinking deep into his bones and reached for his medicine drawer. As he popped a few tablets into his mouth, he found himself envying his assistant, his youth and his privileged carelessness.

Tom had used the moment to move behind him, sliding his fingers over his temples and beginning to massage in small circles. 'Maybe if you transfer some of the work onto the computer, it will go a bit quicker,' he offered, not for the first time. Tom was aware that technology was a challenge for the old man, but that is why he was there, to help.

'You know I don't use the computer much; I really just check my email on it. But when it comes to really working, some things are best done the old-fashioned way,' Mark said, giggling – he imagined this must have sounded like quite the excuse to his assistant.

For what may have been the first time, Tom wasn't listening to the words of his mentor. Instead, his attention was being pulled elsewhere. The reverend's computer, the subject of their conversation, made a small noise, a slight clicking as though cooling down, indicating it'd been used recently.

This wasn't the first time that the young assistant had caught the reverend in a lie. He had a sneaking suspicion that the man was actually quite familiar with computers, but why would he hide this? Tom was his trusted assistant. They had built a strong bond. Tom had even begun forming a bit of an emotional connection, one a bit stronger than was encouraged, no doubt. Secrets had not been part of their relationship, or at least, Tom had thought not. And even though he was young and had a lot to learn, and even had a little trouble controlling his temper – 'a symptom of his youth,' Mark had often said – he felt certain in his decision to satisfy his desire for some answers, which meant getting access to the reverend's computer.

'You're thoughtful,' Mark said after opening his eyes, bringing himself out of the trance brought on by the pleasant massage and noticing the silence.

Tom moved to lean on the desk, standing face to face with him, and Mark stretched out his hand, letting it slide down the intimate parts of his assistant.

While Tom was getting dressed, Mark, still half-naked and relaxing, was thinking about the fact that the boy seemed to have something different from the others, something that didn't disgust him and bring about the hatred that he usually found rising up from within. Was it that the boy had a strong character, reminding Mark of himself in his youth? He didn't know.

Despite his confusion around his apparent infatuation with his assistant, however, he was certain about one thing: he was feeling a level of affection towards Tom that he had never felt towards anyone else, except Simon. And he was more than certain the young man had loving feelings towards him.

That being said, his assistant wasn't enough to satisfy his lust, but there was no reason for the young man to know this. Some things were better unspoken. Mark didn't see this as withholding information so much as evidence of his professionalism.

* * *

Chris was sitting on the grass in the small garden in front of the school, the familiar feeling of déjà vu coming over him as he saw, just a few steps ahead of him, Lina, sitting with her back to him.

Just like last time, and every day after school, her black hair had been let down, releasing its waves to be moved by the wind. Chris smiled and felt the need to go talk to her again, but when he tried to stand up, his limbs wouldn't respond. Panic seized his body in an instant, leaving him stuck to the spot, but at least he had his favourite view in front of him. That hair felt like it could make him forget just about anything.

Chris decided to call out to her. 'Lina …' he said, barely above a whisper. The girl just sat there, and Chris could now see that she was trembling. She eventually turned to face him, revealing a face wet from crying. She had saved him before, and now it was time for him to save her.

He tried again to move but couldn't quite do it, and the desire to do something to help began growing sharply inside him – he felt a need to help her. Then, suddenly, his mission was interrupted as a strong hand came around him and covered his mouth. The smell of the hand's perfume, something that was all too familiar, burned his nose and eyes as goosebumps ran up his arms. He didn't have to turn to recognise his attacker; he knew who it was – it was him.

He wiggled and thrashed, trying desperately to escape, to fight back, but it wasn't enough.

Meanwhile, Lina, his witness, looked on in horror. Tears were falling down both of their faces as he, and then she, did the only thing that could be done – scream. Lina was Chris, and Chris was Lina.

The boy opened his eyes. His bed was wet with sweat, and he was shivering, a pain in his chest as though he'd actually been screaming. Had his parents heard him? He would have to be more careful, or they'd send him to see Father Mark again. He hoped they didn't hear.

He lay there, listening in the darkness. He didn't even bother turning his lamp on; darkness never scared him much. No, he had something worse to fear, something that had been chasing him for the last year, something he didn't know how to escape.

Three years later ...

The scandal around Rita, who had left her husband and daughter, had long since held any interest for the public. Despite all the weird looks and whispering on the street, Ben had been going out, keeping his head up. He'd continued his life's usual routine, no doubt to try and maintain a semblance of normalcy and stability for Lina. David felt it required a great deal of courage. He admired Ben for it.

As for David, things had more or less – save for a few exceptions – slipped back into a state of grey comfort, a sensation of being conveyed forward through his life. It wasn't exciting, but it was movement. Every day he'd go to work at the same office with the same boss who humiliated him whenever he had a chance. The money still wasn't enough. On top of all this, his son had been slipping further and further into a state of silence. He was always isolating himself in his room. He seemed only to want to be by himself. David and his wife tried everything they could to bring him back out, to get him to laugh and smile again, but they seemed incapable of bringing back the carefree son they once knew.

Everybody told them that this was just a phase – normal for kids his age – and that it would go away with time, but for David, it all seemed more serious than an era of pubescence.

A week ago, David and Mary arrived home to find Chris, who had since turned eleven, with a hand covered in blood. He'd perfectly cleaned up the place where the accident had happened and was attempting to put a bandage on, unsuccessfully. Mary and David both panicked and asked him what had happened. Chris explained, very calmly, that he only broke a glass; he hadn't been paying attention while picking up the pieces and had cut himself.

This had seemed logical enough for Mary, but not for David. Something in that innocent accident reminded him of the feeling he'd been getting in his chest, the one that seemed to always be simmering below the monotonous movement he clung to. As a matter of fact, the sensation had slowly increased over the years. It bothered him just a little too often, and he found aggression attempting to bubble up more and more. This certainly wasn't made easier by his boss, who made David feel powerless to change anything about the situation.

There was still the question about where the pain was coming from in the first place, but David knew better than to dig. 'Curiosity, like gossip, has bad roots' was what Father Mark had told him when he was a boy, but something in him did feel like it was trying to come out, one way or another.

On that particular day, David had rolled up his sleeves and was in the process of changing the light in the bathroom. Mary was washing the dishes after the family's Saturday lunch. Chris was probably doing his homework, or playing, maybe even watching television; it was difficult to say lately because no matter what the child was up to, he was always quiet while doing it.

David stepped up onto one of the kitchen chairs, trying to unscrew the old light, but it seemed to have stuck. He felt himself getting angry, angrier than he would have expected, and he put more pressure on it. The result was a broken bulb, pieces of which were now on the floor and in his hand. Blood quickly coloured his fingers, and a curse slipped out of his mouth, which had Mary leave what she was doing to go check on him – he wasn't the type of person to use that kind of language. On the contrary, David had always been known for being quite peaceful and good-hearted.

'Dave! What …?' Mary said, looking at the mess on the floor and trying to read her husband's expression.

'Don't worry about it, Mary. It slipped out of my grip … Just bring the broom. I'll clean up,' he said calmly, and she listened, leaving him alone for a brief moment.

David examined his hand, watching the blood run slowly down his skin, but he had enough awareness about the situation to realise that this was pretty unusual behaviour for him, and he pulled himself away. The pain didn't have him moaning or squirming. On the contrary, he seemed to be enjoying it. He was completely calm, not even twisting his face though his hand was lit in intense sensation.

His mind suddenly fired him back to Chris's accident with the glass and the same serene calm that he'd shown, as though it hadn't even bothered him.

* * *

Today, Mark was excited, like the children off to summer church camp, thrilled at the prospect of some time away from their parents' stern looks. To be honest, he was probably even more excited than them. The reverend had always anticipated this day like a poor man awaiting a promised miracle from the heavenly Father. But the time was nearly upon him. The following day at that same time, he would be outside the city, surrounded by the beauty of nature and responsible for around thirty children of varying ages. For some people, this might sound like a headache, but not for him. No, for him, this was Heaven on Earth.

Mark loved children, and being in their presence nearly twenty-four hours a day for three days was pure happiness for him. Too bad, of course, that something so nice would come to such a quick end, but harmony was never eternal, and he at least had his stolen moments of similar happiness any time he had to help a naughty child brought to his office by concerned parents. But for now, he had tomorrow to look forward to.

Preparations were more or less done, and all there was to do was wait. He was in the process of putting his desk in order when someone knocked on the door.

Without waiting for an invitation, Tom came in and brightened up the room with his smile.

'The father of one of the campers is here and wants to talk to you. It seems there's been some kind of unexpected issue ... I didn't really understand,' he said without the slightest clue as to the response that was to follow.

The expression on Mark's face darkened, like storm clouds had blocked out the light of his eyes.

'What is this nonsense? Backing down at the last moment? Impossible!' He came around his desk and headed for the door, angrier than ever.

'One child less means less to worry about – it doesn't sound so bad, I think,' Tom tried, using the calmest voice he could find. As far as he was concerned, it really was a relief. But, then again, there were a number of things he didn't understand, including why he wasn't permitted to join the other reverends at the camp until the following year. Mark had insisted that he was needed at the church while the others were away, which did make sense – someone had to take care of the place. But as flattered as the young man was to be trusted with such a huge responsibility, the camp sounded fun, and his young soul was thirsty for entertainment – he would go in a heartbeat. There were a few hours of lectures a day, and then all the kids would go and play, and he'd have a few lovely afternoons and evenings alone with his mentor. Picturing it this way, however, only served to rouse his frustrations over not being able to go – it wasn't fair!

Mark had left the room with a sharp exhale and a slam of the door, leaving Tom on his own. The young man bit down angrily on his full pink lip, trying to control his emotions. His gaze, not really focusing on anything, swept the room for something that might help get his mind off of things, stopping abruptly on the reverend's personal computer. A thought he'd tucked away for some time suddenly spiked into his mind – he wanted to see what kinds of things Father Mark deemed worthy of being done on a computer, as well as worthy enough for a lie. This was the first time he'd ever been left alone in his office. The time was now. The room would be locked while he was away, and who knew when the opportunity might present itself after that.

Not to mention, the anger he was feeling over not going was helping him justify his decision – he moved quickly. He locked the door and, literally tiptoeing, went to the desk where he sank into the soft chair. His hand, slightly shaking from the adrenaline, slid the mouse across the wooden surface of the reverend's work station. It turned out that there were a lot of folders, each one holding many more. Nothing seemed particularly out of the ordinary. Sure, he lied about using the computer – he clearly did so a lot – but it ultimately looked like a reverend's desktop. The titles of the folders were even based on religious themes. Even so, he chose a folder at random, just for the sake of checking – over the years, he'd managed to work himself up with a bit of paranoia.

He clicked on a folder named 'Where is the Almighty now?', and to his surprise, he found that it contained a video. A mere second after having pressed play, his eyes went wide and his mouth slowly slacked open without his knowing. His face went pale, and he slapped his hands over his eyes.

Father Mark was standing face to face with Ben, who, despite the dark circles under his eyes, felt more or less fine. Truth be told, he'd pulled himself together a long time ago, for Lina's sake. He was, however, still single. The priority was to keep food on the table – there wasn't a lot of time left for women.

'Father, forgive my interruption, but I've got a lot on my plate and now was the only time I could make it over. My daughter slipped in the bathroom yesterday and broke her leg.' Ben nervously ran his fingers through his hair and exhaled. 'I'm sorry, but she'll have to skip this year's camp. I just hope she'll be well enough for the start of school.'

Father Mark was slowly shaking his head. 'My son ...' he said, putting his hand on Ben's shoulder. 'You know that every struggle is just an obstacle on our path that's waiting to be overcome! And I am here to guide you. Listen to my recommendation.' At this, Ben was certain he felt the man's grip tighten. 'Don't stop the child. Let her join us. You can then use the time to wipe away the fatigue and sorrow from your face. Lina deserves her father to welcome her back with a smile.'

'But …' Ben could tell his face was giving away his confusion, even though he was actively trying to cover it up so as not to appear ungrateful. 'She has a cast on. She can barely walk, and she needs special care. I can't ask that of you …'

At this, the reverend removed his hand from Ben's shoulder. It felt like he was taking a blessing away. Ben got even more nervous, not wanting to upset the holy man.

'Care is at the core of the religion! You, as a religious man, should know this well.' There was reproach in the reverend's words. 'The child will be out in nature, together with friends who can distract her from dark thoughts, and most of all, she will be in safe hands. You can relax and rest knowing she's well and recovering.' At this last, a smile spread on the reverend's face.

Ben smiled back nervously. 'Well, that does sound good—' He couldn't finish whatever he was going to say as Mark's hand came back down to clap a firm pat back on Ben's shoulder.

'Great! It's decided. The bus leaves at 09:00 tomorrow morning, from here.'

* * *

The morning arrived, but it didn't wake Chris – he was already waiting for it with open eyes. In fact, he hadn't closed them all night. He'd probably skip breakfast as well as his stomach was tied like a knot. For his parents, this was just another day with nothing but the usual work and things to be done. But for Chris, this was the day he would leave for church camp. The only thing holding him together was the thought of Lina; his good friend was fated to the same destiny. Time had brought them closer together, and more often than not, they would be together, sitting and talking in the school garden.

Chris had grown up, as had Lina, and so continued an age gap that their peers gave them a hard time over. This only brought them closer, this and the fact that they were both outsiders, outsiders with the same unpleasant feeling constantly at the back of them, torturing them. They didn't really talk openly about the secrets they each had buried deep down in their child's hearts, but they could feel their hearts beating in the same sad rhythm.

That morning, as though determined to go against Chris's desire, time seemed to fly extra fast. When they were finally at the front door, his mom helped him put on his backpack and shoes. Both his parents exchanged a few words then that caught his attention.

'I heard from a colleague at work that Ben's daughter, Lina, had an accident. Apparently, she broke her leg,' Chris's dad said.

His mom let out a compassionate exhale. 'Poor Lina, and poor Ben – bad luck just doesn't leave his side. To be a parent and be powerless against your child's sorrow is a terrible feeling,' she said, proceeding to make sure they weren't forgetting anything. 'And now Lina will have to stay home. Poor girl, a little fun would have done her some good.'

'At least she'll have next year. It's not the end of the world,' Chris's father said – his mom did have a tendency to be a bit overdramatic. Then his dad went quiet, seeming to have fallen into a sudden thought.

Chris's mom hurried him and his dad through the door and locked it behind herself, proceeding to sink into her own world of thoughts afterwards. Nobody noticed Chris's pale face or his silent shock. What was he going to do? The only person who was able to comfort him through the nightmare wasn't going to be there with him. He wouldn't make it on his own, not this time, not again …

The family spent the drive in silence. When they finally reached the church, there was a massive crowd out front. Parents were standing around with their children, some helping to load things onto the bus. Laughter and chatter filled the air with a sort of electricity. Some people had already started boarding the bus.

Mary, who had been holding her son's hand since they'd left the car, turned to look at him. 'Sweetie, are you alright? You're sweating.' Her face turned to that of a medical professional, something which Chris had often poked fun at her for. 'Chris …' There was panic in his eyes.

In his turn, David turned and noticed his son as well. The child was breathing so quickly that it looked like he was struggling for air.

This wasn't Chris's first time experiencing whatever this was – he knew the symptoms – but this must have been the first time it was happening with his parents around. He wasn't sure if the attack had a medical name or anything, or if it was even a real thing. He didn't know if it happened to other people or not – there were a lot of things he didn't know, after all.

Meanwhile, his parents' worried voices sounded distant and muffled, and he could feel his own heart thumping with such force he thought it might actually pop out of his chest. Like a mirage, among the crowd of people, he saw Lina standing there with crutches and a cast on her leg, supported by her father.

This was exactly the sip of air Chris needed. His sight and hearing started clearing up. Maybe there really was someone up there who, on rare occasions, looked out for him.

* * *

David assumed his place behind his work desk, but his mind was far away. He could still see his son's eyes, frightened, looking like they were trying to say something. Both he and Mary were seriously disturbed by the sudden onset of the panic attack. But as suddenly as it had appeared, it was gone. Even though they asked Chris some questions afterwards, they didn't get any answers. Right before he climbed the bus's stairs, David stopped his son and pulled him into a hug.

The feeling in his chest was once again making itself known – David was beginning to blame himself for not being able to understand it. At that particular moment, it was like an aggressive ocean wave collapsing directly over his head as a budding anger rose up within him. It was a feeling he held prisoner, never letting it out, allowing it to eat him alive from the inside.

After the bus had gone, Mary and David exchanged a quick kiss and went their separate ways, each needing to hurry off to work, having no time to discuss what had just happened. But the incident was still fresh on David's mind, and he was sure the same was true for Mary. His mind was digging deep in search of a reasonable explanation, but something felt to be holding him back, preventing him from exploring the full range of possibilities.

He passed the rest of the day in a fog. He couldn't focus, and as a result, he got told off by his boss and was given some extra work that was to be done by the following day. When he finally got home, something different was there waiting for him. Mary had a set of candles lit on the table and two crystal wine glasses were standing there with the dinner. Apparently, his wife was in the mood to celebrate having the house to themselves for a bit.

A smile spread on David's face, but it didn't stay there long. This didn't seem to surprise his wife, however, who came to welcome him with a kiss. She knew he wasn't an expressive person, something that was both a comfort and, on some level, a bit sad for him.

'I hope you're hungry,' she said, using a particularly seductive voice, making the exact nature of her mood all the clearer.

David opened a bottle of red wine and poured some into the glasses. The dinner was delicious, as always, and Mary did most of the talking, as always, but after they finished eating, instead of starting on the cleaning, she invited her husband to follow her to the bedroom. Before they lay down, she held him in her arms, kissing his neck, fingers searching for the button of his shirt. David had given himself over to his wife's tenderness, staying still with eyes closed, trying to shut his thoughts out, if only just for a moment, to simply enjoy.

She began kissing his chest when she got his shirt off, her mouth moving with growing passion. His eyelids instinctively shot open then, like he was stung. In front of them was their wardrobe with body-length mirrors on the doors. David saw his reflection, fixing his gaze on it. He was supposed to feel passion, but he wasn't feeling anything, or at least, he wasn't feeling passion. His stomach was upside down, and his thoughts were chaotic. His reflection showed a man who didn't seem to have control over himself. And yet, he closed his eyes again, lifted his wife up and brought her to the bed where he was to fulfil his duty.

* * *

After arriving at the small two-floor hotel, which was reserved entirely for the group, located outside town in the hills, the three reverends headed for their rooms. Father Mark was feeling impatient to refresh himself with a shower after the hour-long bus ride.

65

With laughter and a lot of chatter, the children all paired off with the person they'd be sharing a room with. Of course, everyone knew that only boys could stay with boys and girls with girls. It was fairly easy for them to pair up. All the children knew each other – apart from attending church together, they all went to the same school.

Everyone got their keys and was shown to their rooms to rest and get settled. Father Mark had already announced that they were all to gather in the garden in an hour for the first lesson.

The reverend's excitement was mixed with boredom. Countless times he's had to stand before people and repeat the same stupid things about the Creator, again and again. He was sick and tired of it, but he also knew that this was his job, and he was going to do it until the end of his days. All the more reason to be grateful that Father Simon had taught him how to properly benefit from his position. Because of this, everything seemed a bit more bearable.

He changed his clothes, even though it was likely that nobody would notice – the clothes of a reverend usually didn't vary much from piece to piece. But he added his special touches here and there – little known to most, Mark did enjoy his vanity.

Before he left the room, he decided he'd spoil himself a little. This trip was, after all, a holiday for him. Sure, he and his colleagues would have plenty of fun after night fell, with expensive old whiskey and whatnot, but why not start the fun a little earlier? After all, he still had a long, boring lecture to get through about the greatest fairy tale of all time – the Almighty. At least it seemed to make more sense when he presented it to the children – they were used to fantasy stories – but when he had to repeat it to adults, sitting there as they nodded their understanding, absorbing every word, it was unbearable agony for him.

Mark pulled a little bottle from his inside breast pocket and took a sip from the burning liquid it held – hundred-proof.

After the stimulating little kick, the day didn't turn out so bad, and it came to an end surprisingly quickly. The children were quiet and disciplined, but he knew that once they were released, they would start running up and down like little demons. They were his Heaven and Hell, if such places did exist – Mark doubted it. To him, these were terms invented to keep the blind blinder, chained in the slavery of faith. He himself didn't often use the terms in his mind and other private spaces.

The night fell, and so came off the holy demeanour and masks of the reverends. 'Ignorance costs dearly!' was Mark's famous phrase, which he used often when surrounded by colleagues, after a lot of alcohol, of course.

And on that night, after the alcohol had blurred his mind, he was feeling more powerful than ever – he was feeling almighty! He left the room where the other two reverends were finishing their bottle and walked down the corridor. His feet would bring him to the right place, he believed.

* * *

Chris was slowly making his way down a narrow corridor of the hotel. The lectures had finished a little bit ago, and they had all been sent off before returning in some hours for dinner and then a movie.. Chris, however, had no appetite nor desire to play with, or even to talk to, anyone at all, save for Lina.

Lina was the only reason he felt any sense of comfort in being there, yet he hadn't seen her much at all. She had skipped the morning lecture, which didn't really surprise anybody given her condition. In fact, everyone was confused as to why she'd come in the first place as her cast would keep her from all the fun. Only Chris knew that she didn't actually want to be there, same as him, but she had no choice … same as him. And now she was missing.

Chris was worried, and her absence was affecting him in that moment more than ever. He headed to her room, keeping the sleeves of his T-shirt down despite the summer heat.

It wasn't long until he came to her door, number thirty-three, and knocked – there was no answer. He was suddenly even more worried; if she wasn't in her room, where could she be, and why hadn't she gone to the lecture then? He knew she must be somewhere nearby as she wouldn't be running away into the woods with that cast.

Chris knocked a second time. 'Lina?' he called, but still no response. 'Lina, are you there?'

Instinctively, he reached for the door handle. It opened, which meant there was someone there. The boy walked in, a bit uncertain as he looked around the small rooms. One of the beds was empty, but on the other was his friend.

Lina was covered with a blanket, crying like she couldn't take a breath. Realising she was alone in the room, he shut the door behind him and walked in boldly. He rushed to her bed and sat. Lina seemed not to have noticed that anyone had even come in.

'Lina …' the boy said softly, her name coming out like a whisper. He stretched out his little hand to caress her. It was only when he touched her that she seemed to notice him, her body going rigid. She started screaming, trying to pull herself back, away from him.

She pulled the blanket over her head and began waving her hand in front of her, blocking herself from him. This unexpected and, most of all, scary reaction frightened the boy at first, but he quickly pieced it together that something was wrong; something must have happened because his friend would never treat him like this.

'It's Chris! It's me. Lina, it's me!' He continued repeating this until, eventually, she finally stopped, blinking with her wet eyelashes and seeming to see him for the first time. She then let her arms drop to her sides, her face twisted in agony, and fresh tears began rolling down her face, which was already red from crying.

'Chris …' she said, only managing a mumble.

The boy was confused and scared at the same time. His heart hurt seeing Lina like this, but he still couldn't understand what could have led to it.

'What's wrong?' he asked, though he had a feeling he wouldn't get an answer. Something had definitely happened to her, something worse than her broken leg. She shook her head, refusing to talk. She began to stare blankly ahead as though refusing to think as well. 'You know you can trust me with anything – you can tell me anything ...' he continued to insist; he knew he could only help her if he knew what had happened.

He needed to see her face calm again, with her beautiful smile spread wide. He wanted to see her wavy black hair and for it to have its soothing effect on him. Instead, his eyes followed her hands. Her lips seemed unable to make enough room for words, only enough for moaning. At first, he thought she was crying, but then he saw her hands clenching in her lap.

Chris's expression changed; something in him told him he was about to see something he wasn't ready to see. Lina was in pain – it was clear now. He didn't take any more time to think. He took the edge of the blanket and lifted it a little. There was blood, not a small amount either. He froze as his mind looked for an explanation, but there were none available, only blood, pain, rage, helplessness, and agony.

Chris quickly stood and headed for the front door, double-checking that it was properly closed and locked. He then grabbed the chair by the table and propped it up under the handle – he'd seen that done in the movies and was satisfied that the knowledge had actually proved useful.

Finally feeling they were safe, for the moment at least, it was time to take care of Lina. The boy took a white towel that he found folded on the table, grabbed a water bottle and went to the bed where Lina was sitting, now shaking.

This was yet another moment in a string of unfortunate moments that connected them. Chris worked, wondering where their heavenly Father, their protector, was at that moment.

* * *

It was nearly the end of summer; only a few days separated David from his son's first day of school. He couldn't wait for Chris to go back, where hopefully studying would keep his mind occupied, away from whatever was bothering him and had caused that panic attack. Both he and Mary couldn't find an explanation for the sudden spike of panic on top of Chris's other odd behaviours. They were hoping Father Mark would have been able to help and that the summer camp would have made an impact, but Chris had come home all the quieter – it seemed like nothing had a positive effect on him. Chris's behaviour was beginning to truly frighten them.

On Saturday, after a delicious lunch of mashed potatoes, steak and salad that Mary had whipped up for them, David decided to do something different that afternoon. Instead of the family gathering together on the couch to watch some comedy, he thought he and Chris could go out back and play some football. Mary was certainly on board to get her son moving and out in the sun.

David knocked on the door to Chris's room, but he didn't wait to be invited in before opening it. There he found his son with a pencil in hand, sitting in front of a piece of paper.

'What are you up to, Chirs?' he asked, smiling as he came around behind to have a look. This wasn't the first time David had found Chris drawing, and it still surprised him, but the fact that Chris was expressing himself in any way at all was incredibly promising. Nobody in the family had a talent for visual arts, but it seemed like Chris was the exception.

When Chris had started reaching for the paper and coloured pencils, David began to think he might be fine, just a quiet boy who chose to immerse himself in his art, but it quickly became clear that this wasn't quite the case.

'Nothing,' Chris shrugged and turned the paper facedown.

This didn't put David at ease, but he didn't want to pressure the kid, so he hurried to change the conversation.

'Do you want to play some football?' The enthusiasm of David's smile didn't get a matched response from his son, which was again just a shrug. 'Come on. It'll be fun – I promise,' he continued, not ready to accept 'no' for an answer.

'Fine,' Chris agreed, not seeming particularly excited.

'Great!' David clapped his hands excitedly. 'Why don't you change into your gym clothes and then we'll head out!'

Chris quickly changed his long trousers for shorts and announced himself ready.

'You'll get sweaty in those long sleeves. Better change into a T-shirt.'

'I'm fine like this,' the child replied, seeming a bit awkward as he did.

'What are you saying? Don't be silly, it's thirty degrees outside.' David was confused.

Chris didn't know if he actually agreed with his father or not, or if he simply didn't want to argue, but all the same, he went back to his wardrobe and picked up a top.

While his son was changing, David used the time to take a quick peek at the drawing left on the desk. He only lifted the edge of the paper a little, but it was more than enough to recognise what he was seeing: a cross coloured nearly black from a pencil pushed firmly into the paper. It was on fire.

'I'm ready,' Chris said, turning to look at him.

David was already one step away from the desk, deep in thought. Recognising he'd need to shake off his pensive look, he cracked into a smile, but it didn't feel like a real expression on his face – he was sure that Chris wasn't convinced.

Together, father and son went out to the back garden, and while Chris was tying up his laces, David noticed something else disturbing: the insides of his son's arms were scratched, as if by a cat. They didn't have a cat, neither did their neighbours. The good mood David had managed to cultivate upon seeing his son drawing had vanished, awakening the pressure in his chest with which he'd become so familiar. Something in him was fighting to be released, to be free, to be able to talk to him freely, but it was stuck somewhere, lodged, still without a voice.

* * *

Tom had just made the afternoon tea and then hurried to leave Mark's office, which surprised the reverend. Usually his assistant looked for an excuse to hang around, little tricks from the young man to get more love and attention – Mark was well aware of the devilish little game. He was certain that Tom felt love for him, and this was what made him so easy to read, but today, he seemed to be in a different sort of mood, given the speed at which he left Mark's office.

It didn't really matter to Mark much in that moment – he actually preferred to be alone. He added his secret ingredient to his tea – whisky – and made sure the office door was locked. Then he got comfortable in his chair and woke up his computer. Leaning back as if to watch a movie, he pressed play on a video. A thin smile spread on his face, illuminated by the light of the screen.

Like most people, he had a hobby – as he put it – and he wasn't ashamed of it. After all, there was nobody to judge him for it, not even the Almighty. 'There's nobody up there, and "up there" has never been. Religion is the creation of the powerful, a game to control the weak,' Mark liked to say, never out loud, of course. He was grateful to count himself among those enlightened, but all the same, he liked to enjoy his 'hobby' in private.

Recording videos was a game for him, something fun. Not to mention, it was much more interesting than simply getting them delivered – the cost of the market aside. By doing it himself, he could watch himself as the main character and re-experience the feeling of the moment, again and again. This was something more than lust – it was power. This feeling always elated him, overtaking him so completely. But the heights of his sensation were reserved for rage, pure hate for weakness, crying and begging. All of it was so pathetic to him. It disgusted him and made him want to be more merciless, to punish the weakness … the same way he wanted to punish *her* – his mother.

Mark was just a child when she abandoned him, throwing him away like a used-up item, back when he needed her love and her protection so much. He didn't remember much else but the pain from her absence.

Then Father Simon had told him the whole truth about his sinful mother, about the ease with which she'd left him to the care of a stranger. She didn't love him, and she never had. Mark owed everything to Simon, who had taken him under his wing with a father's love and taught him about everything he needed to know – power, control, and even intimacy. He could still remember the first time he was intimate with his mentor. He hadn't wanted to be like that with Father Simon, and he was deeply upset, but at the same time, he'd gotten his first and most important lesson: 'The powerful do not cry, do not fear. They conquer. They rule!'

Years after Mark had already grown up, one of his deepest wishes had finally come true. He met his mother again. In fact, she'd found him – he never would have gone searching for her. She appeared at his front door like an uninvited guest, and a vague mixture of emotions kept him from doing what he'd always done in his mind when imagining that moment – send her away. Instead, his silence, a symptom of his shock at actually seeing her in flesh and blood, in front of him, had given her the chance to talk. Her story didn't match the one told by Father Simon.

His father had been a big drinker and had been beating her. Not wanting the same to happen to her child, she went to seek help from the church. Simon offered her a disgraceful proposition in exchange for his help. She, of course, refused, but there, in the middle of that terrible moment, she was desperate. The reverend made another offer, to raise the child as his own and for her to swear that she'd never come back in search of him. She regretted the decision as soon as she'd made it, but she didn't know what else she could do.

Listening to his mother's story, the pain in Mark had turned to anger, nearly aggression. Her weakness had allowed her husband to mistreat her, and it was the reason she allowed herself to be convinced that leaving her child was all she could do. It made him sick. On top of that, she dared to speak against the man who'd raised him and given him everything! Mark told her that she was dead to him and sent her away. That was the last time he saw her.

Now he was a grown man with power that protected him from ever being hurt. He was the one doing the hurting now. He couldn't have been prouder of himself; he turned his life from one of misery to one of bliss.

* * *

As that Sunday's service was about to begin, the church was full of people, all familiar faces. Everyone was huddled in little groups, excitedly enjoying some small talk. Then they'd break and greet some other people, resuming their chatter.

Chris was standing next to his parents, trying to focus his thoughts on the fact that school was starting the following day. He'd hoped to distract himself with this, but it didn't work as school wasn't particularly exciting for him – it was torture. With every passing year, he was becoming more and more shy. A few of his classmates, outsiders like himself, would have been considered social when compared to him. At least he had Lina.

Going back to school for Chris mattered only because he'd be able to see Lina. She lived a bit far from him, and he didn't feel comfortable asking his parents for a ride to spend time with her, so Sundays and school were their only time. Unfortunately, she hadn't accompanied her father to church the Sunday after the camp. This concerned Chris, and he was hoping to spot her.

As he stood there with his parents, waiting for service to start as thoughts of school failed to distract him, he scanned over the crowd of people in search of his friend. He wanted to make sure she had recovered after the camp, that she was trying to forget, and that she didn't have nightmares as he did.

'Hey,' a voice called out from behind. He and his parents turned to see Lina. Her father was beside her, resting a hand on her shoulder.

'Hi, you two. Lina! Done with the cast?' David said, starting a friendly conversation.

'We went to get it off yesterday. Just in time for school,' Ben said, visibly relieved. He was looking better by the day – his smile actually felt organic and genuine.

The adults then started a conversation, and Chris and Lina used the opportunity to move off on their own. They knew they'd only have a few minutes before they'd have to go into the main hall for the sermon, and Lina seemed impatient to share something.

To Chris's surprise, she looked to be doing well – there was a spark in her eyes and colour in her cheeks. He was glad, but he still couldn't shake from his mind the image of her from that afternoon at camp. He couldn't forget her cry, her trembling hands … In any other situation like that, he probably would have been too frightened to do anything, but back in that room, with Lina in such a state, he felt this rush of energy that made him strong, for both of them. He doubted any of his classmates had had an experience like that; they didn't know what it is like to live in a real hell – so he hoped anyway.

'I have big news, but you must swear not to tell anybody!' She kept the full intensity of her gaze on him as she whispered this.

'Of course …' Chris only just managed to say. He had a weird feeling in his stomach. He felt he wasn't going to like what Lina was about to say.

'Chris … I'm not coming to school tomorrow.' Lina looked to be in search of a certain response from him, but he didn't know what he should be feeling, so he just waited. 'I'm leaving tonight. I'm leaving this town forever!' She seemed barely able to keep her voice down – she was evidently happy.

'W-what? … How?' Chris stuttered.

'You should come with me. We can run away together!'

Her face was glowing, contrary to how he felt. For a moment, Chris actually considered that she might have lost her mind. Crazy or not, however, his gut was telling him she was dead serious, and that from then on, everything would change. Nobody wanted a change more than him. Chris dreamed of living somewhere where he wouldn't be forced to go to church, where he wouldn't have to suffer pain and where nightmares wouldn't chase him, where he wouldn't have to suppress the screams tearing him from within. A happy, peaceful life with his family, somewhere where religion didn't exist. But that was just a dream, a fantasy. The reality was different. The change he felt barrelling towards him at that moment didn't feel like a change for good, but he had no power to stop it – he was an eleven-year-old boy.

'My mother called me, Chris. Can you believe that? My mother!' Lina pressed forward, ignoring Chris's lack of response – they didn't have much time left to speak. 'I thought she had abandoned me forever, forgotten about me, that she doesn't love me, but she explained it all to me. She told me that if she'd talked to my father, he would never have let her go, so she had no other choice but to run away. Same as me, Chris! Don't you see? I have no other choice. I can't stay here. I'm so scared here, all the time.' She flinched a bit. Chris understood what she wasn't saying. It was clear she was trying to pass along her enthusiasm to him, to persuade him to go with her. Maybe she saw it as helping, as Chris had helped her.

Her words, however, didn't feel like help to Chris. He knew he couldn't follow her; his vision had gone slightly blurry as his mind began drawing up pictures of what life would be like without his friend.

'She sent me a bus ticket. She sent me two bus tickets, Chris. Come with me!' Lina smiled, care shining through her eyes. 'It's a long way – she lives in the capital city now – but once we're on the bus, we're safe. She'll take care of us! I know you'll miss your parents, but I promise, she'll accept you as her own. We'll be like brother and sister! And when you grow up enough, you can come back here and explain everything to your parents ... Nobody can hurt you when you are an adult.'

It sounded like a fairy tale – happy ending and everything. He just had to be brave enough to embrace this future, this new life. But he couldn't feel even a sliver of the bravery he'd felt when he helped Lina.

'Lina ...' He felt something stick in his throat. He wanted to tell her so many things, like how difficult it would be for him to even breathe with his best friend no longer there.

'Chris ...' It was his mother calling him this time, for him to join them.

'We can talk more after the service ...' Lina assured him, knowing that there was no more time now.

While listening to Father Mark's words, sounding so solemn in the silent hall full of people, Chris could feel his control over himself slipping. His hands were trembling, his palms sweaty, and he could barely contain the sound of his teeth clanging. His face felt red-hot, like it was on fire. He had to focus his eyes on the reverend to try and steady himself. His hands curled into fists, fingernails biting his palms – he didn't know if he was bleeding or not. The only thing he could feel was rage and despair. The man guilty of his suffering was standing there, teaching everyone about love, compassion, faith, and helping one another. He was teaching about the Father. Did the Father approve of what was happening to him? Did their heavenly protector want him to wet his bed and have nightmares? Did the Almighty want the reverend to hurt him or Lina? Maybe he did. Why else would he have given so much power to Father Mark? Maybe all this was normal ...

Then the only problem would be that Chris couldn't seem to take any more of it!

David was listening, concentrating on the reverend as usual, but something made him turn to his son. The child looked somewhat calm, save for his hands squeezing into fists. Again something in himself seemed to wake up. It was angry. It wanted to yell, but it seemed to have plaster over its mouth.

* * *

It was only Tuesday, still the beginning of the week, and there was already a wave of drama sweeping over the town. Lina had run away, and the news was spreading faster than when Ben's wife left. A note was all he'd found, explaining how much she loved him and how much she regretted hurting him, but 'I've been living in a hell' was how she'd put it.

None of it had made sense to her devastated father. Ben knew nothing of the 'hell' his daughter was talking about. As far as he'd known, she was only fourteen and hadn't even seen anything of the real world yet. No matter how much he tried, Ben just couldn't seem to make sense of why the two women in his life had left him. Not to mention, everyone kept telling him how sorry they were for him, and this only darkened his mood.

David couldn't believe the poor man's situation. It all felt like one big injustice. Wasn't it Father Mark who'd said that if the Father took something away it was only to give something better back in return? What good had come back over the last couple of years in the life of this broken man?

However, Father Mark had also once told David, after a church service, that some people are born to be sacrificial lambs. He said they should stop fighting against their destiny as that only creates agony, and they should instead follow the path chosen for them by the Divine. Back then, David had trouble seeing the wisdom in these words. He remembered they had angered him. Then the reverend, no doubt having felt his resistance, explained that not every bit of wisdom could be absorbed by the simple mind. He said that it would take time and knowledge for the truth to be seen, but even that explanation didn't satisfy David's confusion. He didn't know what else to do, however, so he nodded along in agreement. Who was he to argue with a man of the cloth?

In the present, David couldn't seem to get his thoughts off of Ben, which meant he was very distracted that day – it was like everything was going backwards while he awkwardly stumbled forwards along time, upstream. His boss certainly didn't miss the chance to come down on him, threatening that he'd have to stay late if he didn't finish his work.

He watched as 17:00 came and went, and David was still sitting behind his desk, not likely to get up any time soon. After 18:00, he was already completely alone in the office. By a rough calculation, he only needed a couple more minutes and then he'd be able to turn off his computer and head home. That said, he felt strangely at peace. This was the first time he was at the office so late. It was oddly calm when it was empty. It felt nothing like the office he hated so much, nothing like the office with his boss in it.

Suddenly, the sound of steps came up from behind him, startling him – he wasn't alone after all. A not-so-tall woman was standing in the doorway. Noticing her uniform, David could see she was part of the cleaning team. He'd never seen her before, even though he'd worked there for years.

She looked familiar, and she must have felt something similar because she looked back at him intently. He had a name floating around his mouth, but he wasn't sure if he should try it out until, after a brief moment of staring at each other, David remembered his manners and spoke up.

'Daisy?' he tried.

'Dave?' she said in her turn.

He immediately got up, a smile spreading across his face, and went to give her a hug. He wasn't usually so warm when greeting people he was meeting for the first time in the office, but Daisy was one of his classmates, from way back in his long-forgotten school years. She had disappeared after graduation, though, yet there she was. He couldn't believe that after such a long time they'd managed to meet again, and under such circumstances.

'It's been a while,' he said jokingly. 'How are you?'

'Nothing to brag about.' She shrugged.

They were the same age, but David couldn't help but notice that her face looked much older than his. Looking a little closer, it was clear that she was troubled by something, which certainly added to the effect. In fact, the way she held her entire body made it look like she wanted to become smaller, invisible even. To put it bluntly, she looked like life had crushed her.

'How's the family? And work?' David realised far too slowly that he'd asked the wrong questions – subject to the habit of polite conversation.

'I have no family, and the job … is enough to cover my bills,' she said, quickly tucking a loose piece of hair behind her ear.

It was then that he noticed her hands, scars lining the insides of them.

'What happened, Daisy? …' he asked before he could stop himself, pain hanging in his voice. He realised afterwards how direct a question this had been, inappropriate even. They weren't kids anymore – they weren't close friends anymore, but he just couldn't help it. He felt ashamed, and was sure he wouldn't get a response, but to his surprise, she answered. Her voice was low when she did, almost a whisper, and her eyes, locked on his, immediately began shining with tears.

'Not everyone is strong like you, Dave. Not everyone can just carry on. If the Father existed, he would have been my witness to how badly I wanted a normal life. But I couldn't continue after what happened … I'm not like you.'

David found himself breathing rapidly, as if his lungs pulled in air but no oxygen. The whisper inside his head that so often brought about a sense of chaos and confusion was now pulsing as though it was coming to life, waking up, standing up. He felt dizzy. This strange whisper had almost done it, had almost chipped the invisible plaster from his mouth. It was a matter of seconds, and the words that had been muffled all those years would come, pouring, crystal clear.

'What are you talking about?' he asked with dry lips.

The woman looked at him, confusion plain on her face.

'Dave. The big tree in the garden? You must have consoled me a hundred times there. You pulled me out of the river just before I … drowned. You told me I had to keep going. Dave, don't tell me you've forgotten this?'

And that was it. An emotional volcano erupted inside David. Everything came back, everything that had forcibly been pushed down, shoved into the corners of his subconscious, everything he'd tried to delete – it all came back. He was a victim of sexual abuse by one of the reverends at the church, and he wasn't the only one.

David couldn't feel the ground under his feet. The air was tight, and his attempts to get any of it made a wheeze rattle in his throat. He knew this feeling, the panic attacks. They'd stopped in a way once his mind had mysteriously blocked everything that had happened, but now they were back along with everything else. After he'd turned fifteen, he was no longer a subject of interest, and the nightmare, part of it, had stopped, but the memories had kept the hell going, and so his mind had taken care of that in order to save itself. Otherwise, he would have ended up like Daisy.

Daisy's face changed in that moment, falling to one of concern. She pushed her trolley of cleaning supplies to the side and took David's hand, leading him to the nearest chair. Her hand was familiar. Her helping him was familiar. After being seated, he looked down, buried his fingers in his hair and started crying … like he used to. Daisy knelt beside him and looked on the edge of tears herself. He was feeling a personal hell spouting out of him, a hell that Daisy had surely been living every single day.

'I'm sorry, Dave … I'm so sorry that I brought this up. I shouldn't have,' she said, her voice soft and soothing. 'You already have a family. You have a gorgeous son. Just leave the past where it belongs and look forward.'

One word in what she'd just said had stung him in particular – 'son'. He had a son. Yes, he had Chris. The child worried him with his behaviour, behaviour that was, suddenly and painfully, starting to fall into place for David: wetting the bed, aggression coming out in his drawings, and clenched fists during church. All of it was so familiar.

He jumped to his feet, the fully-formed reality suddenly slapping him in the face. Daisy looked at him, jumping at his reaction. His eyes, still wet from the tears, felt as though a fire had lit behind them.

'My Chris …' This was all he said before running out the door, leaving behind his things and leaving Daisy alone to wonder what had just happened.

Nothing else mattered to David in that moment, absolutely nothing apart from getting home as fast as he could.

* * *

It was dinner time, the end of an ordinary day, and Mark was getting ready. Sometimes he longed for something unusual to happen to him just so he could experience something new, something different. The uniformity of routine could do him in from time to time. It was easy for him to get bored, and he always needed something to keep him interested.

As he took his place at the table, which was laden with enough food to feed a few people, the sound of an ambulance pierced the silence and grabbed his attention. Usually, the town was so peaceful and quiet – nothing ever happened there. 'I wonder what it could be,' he mumbled to himself as curiosity started to gnaw at him. Whatever it was, the news was surely going to be spreading around town tomorrow.

Mark turned his attention to the delicious food in front of him and licked his lips, wondering what to start with. He didn't need to pretend when he was alone, so he skipped the prayer. He couldn't go to any of the nearby high-end restaurants as it would hurt his humble image, so he had to recreate the atmosphere at home, to spoil himself as he deserved.

A few plates were spread before him with a number of aperitifs and a large crystal glass filled with dark red wine. After his carefully curated assortment of cheeses, olives and smoked meat, to open his appetite, he would move on to the main course – soft goose meat in a berry sauce.

His phone vibrated like an annoying fly, but he chose not to pay it any attention. He may not have prayed, but his personal time was certainly sacred. He didn't like to be disturbed.

While savouring another mouthful of food, a thought crossed his mind: first the ambulance and then his phone – something different was certainly in the air that evening.

* * *

David arrived home out of breath and covered in cold sweat, but his attention was immediately arrested as the police were parked outside his house. He walked towards his front door slowly, giving himself time to adjust to the situation. Mary appeared then in the doorway with a police officer beside her. His arm was on her shoulder and his face was the picture of sympathy. Her face, on the other hand, was etched by horror. He was looking right at her, but he hardly recognised her. As he looked at her swollen, red eyes, he could feel the tragedy that had already happened. He could feel the shifting transition actively turning his world upside down.

Mary's eyes met David's, and she broke completely. She ran to him, but instead of opening his arms to embrace and console her, he found himself gripping her shoulders and shaking her roughly.

'Speak, Mary! Speak!'

The woman was choking on her tears and noticeably startled by her husband's behaviour. She was completely unable to speak. At that moment, the police officer who had walked her out of the house came up to them. 'Sir, please, I need you to take a breath for me.'

David did so, losing the grip on his wife's shoulder, giving it a small rub with his thumb before taking his hand away. 'I'm sorry to put this on you all of a sudden, but time isn't on our side. Your wife couldn't bring herself to look at the body, so we need you to identify the child.'

It was the type of moment that could freeze a person's blood, one that would leave its mark until the end. Some might ask questions at a time like this: Why me? Why is this happening? What did I do to deserve this? But these never bring answers, only more pain. There is no greater sadness for a parent than attending the funeral of their own child.

After identifying the lifeless body that had once been their son, which had been covered with a white sheet on a stretcher by an ambulance, Mary fell into a numb shock, and David felt a bomb ready to blow inside him. He escorted his wife back to the house. As she set to work organising the funeral, he went out to attend to something urgent. Mary didn't even ask where he was off to. In fact, she seemed not to notice much of anything that was happening around her.

David felt like he was running through a dream, another dimension, one in which he was completely overtaken by pain and a desire to punish. He was moving fast, eyes wild; if foam had been coming out of his mouth, it wouldn't have looked out of place. He sought only one person.

David passed through the entrance of the church, and for the first time in his life, he didn't make the sign of the cross. He rushed into the hall, where Father Mark was presently in the middle of performing a ceremony. All eyes turned back to look at him, the newcomer, who had so rudely interrupted the holy event, but David didn't care – he didn't even care that there would be witnesses. He walked straight up to the altar, pushed the family gathered there aside, and without missing a beat, threw a tightly clenched fist right into the reverend's face.

People exclaimed, screamed, and shouted, and Mark, even though his body was chubby and heavy, fell to the ground. Amongst the chaos that ensued, James, the old cleaner, burst into the room.

'Monster!' David shouted. 'It's your fault – yours and everyone like you! I will destroy this place; I'll burn it to the ground and bury you under it!' He was completely out of control, reaching out his hand to grab the reverend's collar as the man lay flaccid on the ground, a look of dumb confusion on his face.

Once Mark saw the old cleaner, he started shouting orders. 'Call the police! You hear me? Call the police!'

'There will be no justice for you, monster. Hell's expecting you – it's prepared a special place for you.' The words squeezed out of David's tightened jaw.

James ran, but not to call the police. Instead, he went to hold David, trying to get him away. He was old, but David wasn't particularly strong. Adrenalin was coursing through him, but eventually, he surrendered to the force pulling him back. The cleaner had wrapped his hands around him and began whispering so only he could hear, 'Calm down, my brother … calm down … breathe. You must leave now! Listen to me, or danger will come down upon you!'

Somewhere between the anger and the pain, these words made an impression on David, and he let himself be dragged out of the church. Once outside, the old man released him.

'I haven't called the police, but I believe a member of the family has. They'll be here shortly. Even if you leave right away, they'll find out it was you. You better start thinking of a good explanation for when they come to your house,' the old man advised.

David was shivering. 'Explanation? I'll tell the truth! That monster deserves to be punished!' David yelled these last words, a threat he hoped would reach the reverend inside. James slowly shook his head, and with a sad look in his eyes, he spoke:

'And who do you think will believe you? Who will stand behind you? The whole town that goes to church every Sunday? Or perhaps the police to whom you'll only look mad from grief, accusing a respected and well-known man of the church? You are alone in this, and everyone will be against you! Believe me, you will be lucky if they don't have you arrested.'

David frowned, following the logic of the words. As much as he didn't want to admit it, the man had a point. He had no proof – it would be his word against the word of a reverend. He could already see the cold reality – he would lose this battle, and there wouldn't be any justice. The monster would continue to walk amongst the people. He now understood this, but his pain was still throbbing inside of him.

'My family is the victim, not him.' David pointed a finger at the doors of the church while his eyes filled with tears.

'I know. Believe me, I know … But these people are untouchable. The community's judgment and the judgment of the Almighty always float right past them – they're smart. Leave this town. Give yourself a fresh start.

'You have a wife – maybe you can have another child. But don't start something that will certainly destroy you.' James gave David's shoulder a heavy, solemn pat and headed for the entrance of the church to resume his duties, leaving the poor man outside, falling to his knees, devastated.

Unbeknownst to both of them, however, their conversation had a witness. Tom stood, unseen, in the corner of the entrance.

* * *

Mark still couldn't believe what had happened to him. Mixed emotions were threatening to overtake his inner peace. At the bottom of his soul, a place he didn't often care to look, there was fear. He had this fear because he was a victim, and there was nothing that could guarantee that he wouldn't be attacked again. This same fear was simultaneously fueling his anger – victims were weak, and he most certainly wasn't weak! He'd always looked at his own victims with disgust, drawing power from their terror, but now he wasn't the strongest. Even if he wanted to fight back, or at least defend himself, his hands were tied. As a reverend, he was a pacifist – he couldn't show his anger and aggression, especially not in front of a crowd. He had to save face above all else.

'Who the hell does that man think he is?' he hissed under his breath. He was evidently so bold and fearless as to enter the Almighty's house with the intention to hurt him, and in front of people. It was madness; he must have lost his mind, although even the crazy ones had respect for the Almighty and his holy servants.

Mark's mental processing was beginning to give him a headache, something that felt all the worse when paired with a bruised jaw, which he was presently pressing some ice to. Mark couldn't remember the last time he felt pain or discomfort like this. He was accustomed to being the predator, and the fact that he had to take that punch and do nothing about it was sitting in his stomach like a hot ember. He wanted revenge. The one at fault should be punished. Mark was humiliated, and that came with a high price that had to be paid.

The door opened, and before him stood the one person who had a soothing effect on him. Something in the young man's expression seemed twisted, but that didn't seem too odd considering the circumstances; his assistant must have been scared for his beloved mentor. After all the attention from the police officers and the medics, which he found a bit overwhelming, Mark was relieved to see Tom.

Tom came closer, taking hold of the ice pack so the reverend could give his hand a rest.

'How are you feeling?' the young man asked, trying to cover his lack of interest, hoping the reverend wouldn't notice.

Mark looked at him like a toddler seeking attention. 'I feel the way I look – horrible! I've been humiliated in my own home, the house of the Creator. That man will burn in Hell, I'm telling you!' The reverend punctuated the air with a finger, getting a bit too theatrical for Tom's taste.

The young man just raised an eyebrow. 'I heard he was trying to send you there first for abusing his son.' The words came out of Tom's full lips so casually, so innocently, and the reverend's mouth fell open.

'A lie, an ugly lie! They want to disgrace the Father's name!' he said, practically yelling, but his eyes betrayed him. The same eyes Tom knew so well were now confirming the lie, confirming who the reverend really was. Previously, he may have believed him, mainly because he wanted to, but he couldn't unsee what he saw on Mark's computer. He thought what they had was special – he thought it was real, that their love was real … But now he knew he was being naive.

Mark's face went red, and the indignant drama in his eyes turned to something wild – he was angry.

Mark decided, then and there, to defend himself at any cost. He was so fired up he'd completely forgotten about the pain in his jaw. 'You don't believe those lies, do you?' he asked, getting to his feet and on eye level with his assistant. Mark stared, not even blinking, as though he were trying to telepathically convince the young man of his innocence.

'How could I?' Tom said, knowing there was something different in his voice, something dry, something dead – he was being dishonest right to the reverend's face.

Mark, however, was so focused on his situation that little details such as unsaid words simply didn't register to him. He started to pace nervously around his office.

'Obviously, this is a horrible tragedy,' Mark started. 'I will pray for the poor soul of the child, although I have no clue what made him jump off that building. But I do know that people who commit suicide are not welcomed into Heaven. And his father, with these accusations, won't get close to the heavenly kingdom either. Does he even realise with whom he's dealing? He should consider himself lucky that I don't press charges against him.'

'Why don't you press charges?' Tom interrupted, curious. 'You're hurt, and you're scared, no doubt – he could attack again.' He was enjoying teasing his mentor, making him sweat and cover his lies as they left him.

'Because, my dear Tom,' Mark said, getting intimately close him, 'I am a reverend. I represent the Creator. I can't harm anyone!' His voice was soft now, emotional.

'Of course you can't. You have to turn the other cheek,' Tom added, playing his role well.

'Exactly! Ah, Tom, I wish everyone could see me through your eyes,' Mark said, wrapping his hands around Tom's waist and pulling him in for a shallow hug.

These moments used to delight the young assistant, but not anymore. That was a dream he couldn't fall back into now that he was awake. A plan started forming inside Tom's head, a plan promising justice.

Three months later ...

David was making one final order before quitting for the day.

The office he was in was a new one, and the home he'd go back to was new as well. In fact, the town his home was in wasn't the same one in which he'd grown up and lived all his life. David and Mary opted for a fresh start – it was that or collapse from grief. The sorrow of losing their only child was one thing, but to continue living in the same house and walking the same streets would have only served to feed their despair.

That, however, wasn't the only reason they'd left. A day after the situation at the church, he received a call from his boss. After offering his condolences, he advised David that they had to let him go, effective immediately. After a bit of pushing towards the real, unofficial, reason for his termination, he was told that there wasn't room on the team for someone who wasn't open to religion.

This wasn't the only bit of the church's influence to rear it's head. After the loss of his son and his job, David was called into the police station to make a statement about his act of aggression towards the reverend. They didn't ask about his son and what had happened there. It was clear where their priority was. The story David presented about the sexual abuse wasn't well received. The police even managed to twist the statement in such a way that made it sound like the boy had been triggered by family issues – namely, David's evident aggression.

The people about town made no effort to hide their staring and glaring. They had no apparent problem with pointing and whispering as they passed. Some of them even shook their heads, speaking openly about their disapproval of David 'lying' about the reverend and the church. Some others gave looks of sympathy, as though they understood what they were going through. That was worse somehow – nobody understood.

The stress and grief of the whole situation had even taken a toll on Mary's physical health and appearance. The poor woman couldn't get out of bed for days after everything had happened. There was no life for them in that town, no future. The spontaneous decision to move came when David remembered the advice of the church janitor, James. He'd recommended getting out of town, and that's what they decided to do.

Three months later, David and Mary had their house on the market. They'd found themselves a small flat in a bigger city, far from their town. Both husband and wife were fighting their own personal battles. For Mary, a mother who'd lost her son, the grief wiped out her ability to think clearly for few moments at a time, sometimes longer. On the other hand, David was fighting on two fronts, the grief over his son and the grief and anger over his past.

One thing that held them together through it all, however, was their shared battle, the battle for justice. There was no way to get their son back, but they could seek to avenge him and bring punishment to the monster who deserved it. Their case was popular, and they were able to support many children and parents, but waging a war against the church was another thing entirely – the outcome of that battle was already decided, and it hadn't even started yet.

David was zipping his briefcase, ready to leave the office, when his computer made a sound. This told him two things: he'd forgotten to switch off his computer, and he just received an email. This latter thing was a bit odd, considering everyone was wrapping up for the day. So, being curious, he went to have a look.

David set his briefcase on the floor and sank back into his desk chair to check his mailbox. His eyes, tired and red from constant exhaustion and simultaneous lack of sleep, were now staring into the monitor. The email appeared to be anonymous. The address of the sender was hidden – clearly a virus.

He was just about to delete it when a voice in his head, despite all logic, told him to open it. Though, if he jammed up his work computer with a virus, he'd be in a decent amount of trouble.

'Maybe I'll just wait until I get home, to open it on my personal computer,' he mumbled to himself, but then he clicked, his finger going for it before he had time to reconsider. To his surprise, and relief, it didn't appear to be a virus. There was a small bit of text and a video attached.

'The Almighty would want justice.
With this proof, nobody can shrug you off
anymore.
Don't lose your faith in the Creator; the
Divine is not sinful, people are!'

David could feel the familiar sensation of his blood beginning to boil and the sudden return of the pulsing in his head, blurring his vision with little black dots. He never wanted to hear the word 'Almighty' again, ever! He immediately wanted to know who'd sent him the email, the nasty joke.

David, with trembling fingers, was ready to delete the email when he remembered the video. He'd already come this far, he figured, so he might as well finish what he started, even though he was fully expecting to see some nauseating religious propaganda designed to lure him back to the church.

He opened the video.

David groaned and immediately pushed himself back away from his desk. His body convulsed, and the food he enjoyed for lunch became nothing more than a dirty spot on the floor. Somewhere, however – though his fingers were currently covering his mouth to keep him from vomiting more and tears were blurring his vision – there was a voice whispering, *'Victory!'*

Three weeks later, this was all the media seemed capable of talking about. On every channel and radio station, the same thing was ringing out: 'Reverend of a small town arrested for abuse. Many more trials to follow with other cases surfacing in neighbouring towns and elsewhere.' The phone lines at the police station had never been busier – they didn't stop ringing for days.

One television was switched off. It belonged to a home that, until recently, had been filled with sorrow, but was now opening up to hope. David sat on the couch with Mary laying her head on his shoulder, both in silence as a jumble of feelings flooded through them. Yes, justice had been served. There'd been a victory of good over evil. The light had triumphed over the darkness, but at what price?

Notes from the Author

When I set out to write *The High Price*, my intention was never to criticise or target any institution, religion, or belief system. This book is a work of fiction, and its purpose is to shed light on a broader issue – one that affects countless people in different ways. Many individuals struggle in silence, whether due to anxiety, depression, loneliness, or various forms of abuse, often feeling unable to seek help or fearing that their voices will go unheard.

Through this story, I want to emphasise the importance of societal awareness and the need for a more compassionate, observant community where no one feels invisible in their pain. The setting and storyline I chose are entirely fictional and only inspired by many well-known films that explore similar themes.

104

About the Author

Lora Kay is a self-published author. Born and raised in Bulgaria, she later moved to the United Kingdom, where she studied Psychology at the University of West London. She balances her time between working and writing, pursuing her passion for storytelling.

Lora finds great joy in creating manuscripts that explore the complexities of human emotions. Her stories often carry a darker tone, offering a lens into the raw and unfiltered aspects of life. Her love for books has always been a driving force – not just as a reader, but as a writer committed to exploring themes that spark reflection and raise awareness of important issues.

Her books are available worldwide through Amazon, Goodreads, Waterstones, Barnes & Noble and more.

Connect with Lora: webpage **lorakaybooks.com** and Instagram **@lora_kay_writer**

www.ingramcontent.com/pod-product-compliance
Ingram Content Group UK Ltd.
Pitfield, Milton Keynes, MK11 3LW, UK
UKHW020342020825
461464UK00005B/185